BITTERSWEET DWELLING

Paige Turner

WESTBOW
PRESS®
A DIVISION OF THOMAS NELSON
& ZONDERVAN

This is a work of fiction. All of the characters, names, incidents, organizations, and dialogue in this novel are either the products of the author's imagination or are used fictitiously.

WestBow Press books may be ordered through booksellers or by contacting:

WestBow Press
A Division of Thomas Nelson & Zondervan
1663 Liberty Drive
Bloomington, IN 47403
www.westbowpress.com
844-714-3454

ISBN: 978-1-6642-1739-3 (sc)
ISBN: 978-1-6642-1741-6 (hc)
ISBN: 978-1-6642-1740-9 (e)

Library of Congress Control Number: 2020925390

Print information available on the last page.

WestBow Press rev. date: 02/10/2021

Dedication

I dedicate this book to my Father and Mother who are amazing gifts from God. My Mother lovingly and patiently taught me to be kind to others and to help those in need. My Father encouraged me to be strong and to defend myself when necessary. I am thankful to them both for teaching me to trust in Jesus and His great love.

Acknowledgement and Thanks

lthough many friends and family have encouraged me along the way, I could not have completed this book without my husband and his patient love for me. I want to acknowledge him for supporting me and helping me in every step of the way. He spent many hours proofreading and helping me edit the book. I could not have completed it without his computer savy intelligence.

Preface

ometimes God uses the simple things of life to allow us a glimpse
of His truths, but other times He reveals Himself through the
dramatic, the shocking, and even the unthinkable. Life's events
can drive us to our knees in desperation or lift us to new heights of joy
and celebration. All too often while living our lives in the moment, we
fail to step back far enough to see the finger of God weaving Himself
into the unique fabric of our life.

Throughout my childhood, I enjoyed writing poetry, and short
stories. My poems and short stories were often inspired by the people,
the experiences, and events that were part of growing up. As I grew up,
I began writing my thoughts and the days events in diaries and journals.
When I would share with people how I was raised, and how my family
left the modern world of the 1960's to became Mennonite, I would often
hear "you need to write a book" in response.

For twenty years I knew that God wanted me to write a book. I
made time to write eight chapters but after that, I would start to write
more and then stop again. I didn't make it a priority in my life. I kept
busying myself by doing all sorts of very good things. I was part of our
church drama team, sang in the choir, and helped with youth group
activities. I gardened and canned, I entered my flowers in fairs and won
ribbons, and my husband and I traveled the USA.

It was during the early stages of 2020 and the Corona virus shut-
down, that God finally got my full attention regarding writing this
book. He revealed to me that doing good things can be the wrong
things, if I wasn't doing what He was calling me to do. He knew that
my experiences in life could be used to inspire, encourage, and bless

others. I began writing the first book of a planned four book series. It is my hope that God will use this simple act of obedience to bring as much joy and encouragement to those who read it, as it has given to me while writing it.

CHAPTER One

Once Again

I t was the year 1963 on a cold February morning in Indiana, and everything was covered with snow. The sunshine made the town of Kirksville sparkle like a beautiful winter wonderland. Sandra had only a short drive to her doctor's appointment that morning. She loved the snow, and her thoughts wandered back to her childhood memories of sledding and ice-skating when she was a child. When she arrived at the clinic, she couldn't help but reach down for a handful of snow to make a snowball, and she threw it at the light pole. She didn't mind that she had to park in the very back of the parking lot. She enjoyed the walk through the newly fallen snow, and made a fresh path through it to the entrance.

After checking in at the front desk, Sandra took a seat in the waiting room. She noticed the middle-aged lady sitting next to her was obviously pregnant. Sandra nervously looked around the room, and started biting her fingernail. The lady looked up from her magazine, and stared at Sandra with curiosity. "Hi. I couldn't help but notice that you seem anxious. Are you expecting your first child?" she asked with a smile. "Hello. No. This will be my third child. How many will this be for you?" Sandra asked. "This will be my fifth, and my last," she answered, with a laugh as she rubbed her tummy. "How wonderful. I would like to have at least six children but this will be my last also," said Sandra, with sadness in her voice, "I don't mean to sound ungrateful. I realize there are many women who want children, but aren't able to have any." Just then, a nurse called the lady's name. As she stood to follow the nurse, she told Sandra that three children should keep her very busy.

A few minutes later, a nurse called Sandra's name, and led her to an examination room. While waiting to be seen by Dr. Woods, she watched the big snowflakes fall against the window. She thought about how she had put the appointment off long enough. Being over two months along now, she shouldn't wait any longer. She dreaded even going back to see him, because of what he said to her after delivering her second child. He advised her to have her tubes tied after she had a cesarean with her first baby, and he told her the same thing, when she had her second baby by cesarean also. She refused to listen to him again. How could she have only one child, when she wanted a house full of them? After the second baby, he insisted that she must not have any more children because it would be too risky to have another C-section in the same place again. "I don't want to see you back a third time, young lady. Do you understand," was Dr. Woods' orders. Now here she was pregnant for the third time and feeling guilty.

Once again, she refused to listen to her doctor's advice. She knew he would be angry. "What does it matter if he blows off a little steam," she thought, "It's my body, after all, and I want this child more than anything. I shouldn't feel guilty for that." She was tired from working all week at the factory on the assembly line and just wanted to get this appointment over with and go home to her husband and little ones. She knew her husband David would have supper ready soon and little Derek and Ruthann would be anxiously waiting for her hugs and kisses.

Sandra had just fallen asleep when the door swung open. It startled her, and for a moment, she forgot where she was. When she saw the look on Dr. Woods' face, it expressed exactly how he felt. "Not you again," he blurted out, irritated just to see her there. "Sandra, I told you that I didn't want to see you in here again." Looking down and nervously wringing her hands, she gave a big sigh, and then looked up at him. "Look, Doctor Woods, I know. I know! Just hear me out. Please. I have always loved kids, and I wanted a passel of them. You told me that I have narrow hip bone structure, therefore I can't have them naturally, only by C-section. How do you know that a woman can't be cut the third time in the same place for it? Have you had a patient with that scenario before?" asked Sandra, passionately. With his hands on his hips and an angry look on his face, he stepped closer to her. "No, and that is beside the point! Most of my patients listen to me and take my advice! It will be very difficult for the incision to heal, the uterus is weak so it could literally tear open, and then there is the scar tissue--" Sandra interrupted him. "So you're telling me that you're scared then? Maybe you aren't sure you can do it," said Sandra, challenging him. Her questions made him furious. "Questioning me and my ability now, are you," the doctor replied, as he defended himself, "young lady, what am I going to do with you? You certainly try my patience," Dr. Woods said, with frustration. He turned around to look at his clipboard. "There he goes with that "young lady" stuff again," she thought. Sandra didn't feel young at all. She already had two children, and worked at the factory for three years. She was barely twenty-three, and the doctor didn't want to see her life endangered in any way. Although she aggravated him with her stubbornness, he was very fond of her. He was a good friend of the family and had delivered her when she was born.

"Okay Sandra, lie down here, and let's take a look at that stomach first," said Dr. Woods, with a sigh. Sandra's stomach had a long horizontal scar that she was very self-conscious of. She wished her skin had more elasticity in it, and that she had the flat tummy she had when she got married. She would gladly do it all over again though. The scar and all that came with it, was more than worth it, to have the little ones she loved so dearly. David assured her many times that she was beautiful, and it didn't matter to him at all. He assured her that he loved her for who she was, not for how her body would ever look. He told her often that she was beautiful inside and out.

Dr. Woods' brows showed concern. As he rubbed his chin, he spoke to her in a more gentle tone. "You know, we can take care of this matter discreetly so you wouldn't have to suffer through this pregnancy," he said quietly." Sandra couldn't believe what she just heard! Anger rose up inside of her, as she tried to find the words to say without chewing him out. "Doctor, I respect you, and even think of you like one of our family, but how could you suggest such a thing?" asked Sandra, insulted by the suggestion the doctor had made. He responded gently once again. "Sandra, I care about you too and that's why I don't want any complications to arise that would put your life in danger. You must understand where I'm coming from. Do you realize that as the baby grows and your stomach stretches, that it will be putting way too much pressure on the old incision? The tissue inside could literally tear. What a mess you've gotten us into," Dr. Woods said, shaking his head in disbelief. There was silence. Somehow Sandra had to make him understand. Tears began to run down her cheeks. "It is not your mess," she replied, "I can go to another doctor if you don't want to deliver this baby." Dr. Woods hated to see her so upset, and knew he had stepped way out of line. He apologized and it was accepted. With that, he just threw up his hands and gave up. "I can see that you are going to go through with this no matter what I say. You know the drill---eat right, get plenty of rest, and no alcohol or cigarettes! You remember the hard time we had getting Ruthann to breathe when she was born. I still say, it was due to your excessive smoking! I thought we were going to lose that little girl. She was in the hospital a week before you could take her home, wasn't she?" asked Dr. Woods, with a scolding tone. Sandra felt very guilty about that, and she wasn't about to put this baby in danger with smoking. "Yes, doctor. She was. I quit smoking. I'll be a good young lady," said Sandra, slowly exaggerating the "young lady." "Getting lots of rest may not be possible though. With my two little ones, my full-time factory job, and housework there's little time left for rest," explained Sandra. Dr. Woods was getting frustrated and began scolding her. "Sandra, if you want this pregnancy to be successful and without complications, for you or the baby, then you have to listen to me this time! Got it?" Sandra hesitated for a moment. "Got it," she sighed. After he left the room, she was feeling physically and mentally tired. She was glad that it was a Friday. David cooked supper on Fridays, and she would get a little more rest during the weekend.

As Sandra put on her coat to leave the clinic, all she could think about, was how to tell David the news. She was glad that the worst was over though. Dr. Woods was the hardest person to tell and it was a big relief that it was done. While scraping the snow off the windshield, her mind went back to how she would tell David that they were going to have a third child. He had plans to buy a larger home and build up a savings account. Their little brick home, in a peaceful housing addition in Kirksville, was nice, but it only had two bedrooms. Derek and Ruthann had to share a room. It was a large room, and they were still very young, so it would be sufficient for a while longer. The spacious kitchen was Sandra's favorite room in the house because she loved to cook and entertain. Their large backyard was fenced-in. The children had a new swing set and a sandbox to play in. Sandra knew things would be crowded in their home for a while, but they would manage just fine.

Finally, she thought, as she jumped into the car. She shivered from the cold as she drove away. Sandra decided that she would just wait a couple days before telling David about the pregnancy. Tomorrow would be Derek's fourth birthday, and she didn't want things to be tense between her and David at his party. She hoped her mother wouldn't be able to detect anything out of the ordinary, or question if there was anything wrong. There would be a lot of family there. The focus needed to be on Derek, not on her. She was convinced that she had a good reason to wait to tell him the news later, and was sure that David would understand why she waited.

As Sandra walked in the front door of their home, she was greeted by shouts of joy from Derek and Ruthann. They hugged her legs with all the strength their little arms could give, but their display of affection almost made her lose her balance. After hugs and kisses, she was free to take off her snow covered boots. She dropped into the lazy boy chair to rest before supper. In an instant, both children were on her lap. Sandra lovingly welcomed their desire to cuddle for a while. She didn't like leaving them with a babysitter, but she had to work to make ends meet and to have the things they desired. As they sat there, she could smell David's fried chicken. It usually made her mouth water, but now it was making her feel sick to her stomach. He made the best fried chicken she ever had, and he was very proud of that fact. The joy of cooking was one of the many things they had in common. They liked planning menus and preparing meals for Sunday lunches. They often invited their relatives and friends to join them.

David entered the living room with a bite of chicken for Sandra to sample. "You look tired, sweetheart. Here's a taste of what's to come for supper," David said, as he held the fork in front of her face. Sandra didn't even want to look at the bite of chicken, let alone taste it. She refused by putting her hand in front of it. "What's wrong? You never turn down a tasty morsel like this. Someone needs to make sure it's good before I serve it," said David, sounding disappointed. Thinking fast, she looked at Derek. "I want to save my appetite for supper. We'll let Derek try it for us," said Sandra, making it sound fun so that he would want to do it. He was more than willing to take part in the little game. David gave the sample to Derek. "Mommy, daddy's chicken is wonderful!" Derek said, still chewing. Ruthann chimed in when she noticed Derek talking with his mouth full. "We aren't 'spose to talk with our mouth open when we eat Derek," she said with a bossy tone. "How can we talk with our mouth closed Ruthie?" Derek asked, with a very serious expression. Ruthann ignored Derek's question. "Daddy's chicken is always yummy," she said sweetly. David and Sandra glanced at each other. They were both trying to hold back their laughter. "Ruthann, I think you meant, "we aren't supposed to chew with our mouth open". Okay with that settled, let's go eat before it all gets cold," said David, trying to compose a straight face. The things the children could come up with, entertained their parents often these days. Derek was four, a year older than Ruthann, but she didn't seem to know that, and would often try to boss him around. He was very easy going, and didn't let his little sister "ruffle his feathers" with her comments.

Disappointment was clearly seen on David's face, as Sandra passed up taking any chicken, when he held the platter out to her. She quickly turned the conversation to the plans for Derek's birthday party. They considered having a full meal for those attending, but when they came up with as many as thirty possible guests, they changed their minds. They decided to only have cake and ice cream. When Sandra asked Derek if he wanted chocolate or white cake for his birthday, he told her that he didn't care, but would really like to have peanut butter cookies too. Her homemade peanut butter cookies were his favorite. She assured him that she would make some in the morning, and that he could have a cake also. Derek hugged her and thanked her for letting him have both because there needed to be a cake to put the candles on. David overheard their conversation. He winked when he told Sandra that Derek could "have his cake and eat it too."

With the little ones put to bed, Sandra and David sat on the couch to watch the evening news. It was their favorite time of day, when they could relax and be alone. They liked to talk about their day, and their plans for the future. This evening Sandra was quiet and seemed distant. David thought it was because she was thinking about her father. Sandra's father, Evan, had not been well for the last year. Lately, he sat at the kitchen table and drank beer most of the day. He was a highly intelligent man who could talk about almost any subject. One of his favorite things to talk about was geography. He could talk about any country and the traditions they have. The radio that he kept on a shelf near him, was on all day long. It wore on his wife's nerves. She often asked him to turn it down, but he had bad hearing, so he didn't hear her. The pain he had from arthritis and other ailments was sometimes unbearable. Sandra believed that her father drank to ease the pain. No one could convince him to go to a doctor or almost anywhere. His wife, Maggie, wanted him to go to a doctor about his coughing, which she was sure, was due to him smoking two packs of cigarettes a day. It was hard for Sandra to see the condition he was in now, because she could remember when he was so strong, confident, and much happier.

"Where are you tonight, Sandy?" David asked with concern. David started calling her "Sandy" ever since their first date. She liked it and thought it was special, because only he called her that. "Huh? Oh, I'm sorry David. I'm just very tired and don't feel so well tonight," answered Sandra. David put his hand on hers. "I knew something was wrong when you passed up my fried chicken at supper. I thought you might be worried about your dad." Sandra sighed, "Yes. I am worried about him. I just don't know what we're going to do about him being so stubborn. Mom is at her wits end with trying to convince him to go to the doctor, and his excessive smoking has her worried too. His coughing is getting worse. Mom and dad were so happy, but these days, they seem to be arguing or not talking at all. I know it's very hard on mom to see dad that way. She says that he talks to himself, and he also has conversations with the radio, David," said Sandra, with raised brows. That made David laugh. Sandra told him that she didn't think it was funny, but then she began to laugh along with him. "He has conversations with his twin brother who is fifty miles away too. Mom told me that she hears dad answering his brother's questions!" Sandra said, trying to be more serious. They finally stopped laughing. "Do you know if he will be here for Derek's birthday party tomorrow?" David asked. "I doubt it. Mom doesn't like to leave him alone at all, so she won't be here long, I'm sure," sighed Sandra. She snuggled close to David, and rubbed her hands through his thick dark hair. "Let's not talk about dad anymore tonight, sweetheart. Let's not talk about anything else right now."

CHAPTER Two

The Birthday Celebration

as she dreaming, or was it real? Sandra thought she heard a baby crying. She woke from a dream about having a natural childbirth in her very own home. She thought about that for a moment, and then she heard the sound again. It wasn't a baby crying. It was Ruthann, and she was calling "daddy, daddy come quick!" David was up in an instant. Just as quick, Sandra was up, and together they ran to the children's room. David ran to Ruthann's bed where she was standing in the middle of it sobbing. He took her up into his arms, and asked her what was wrong. Sandra was trying to comfort Derek, who was just as excited and scared. Both children weren't making much sense at all, but things got quieter when Sandra turned on the bedside lamp. She held Derek on her lap, while David spoke to the children. "We're here with you, and everything is alright. Ruthie, what were you saying about someone being under the bed?" Wiping her eyes, she began to tell her father, what she thought, had happened. "I woke up because I heard something under my bed. It was a soldier and he's still under my bed," she said, pointing. "How do you know it's a soldier Ruthie?" Ruthann's eyes widened with excitement. "Because I saw him stand up, and he had a long gun in his hand." Derek joined in the conversation. "I heard him and saw him too. He walked over to my bed, and then disappeared when you and mommy came in." Ruthann shook her head, "No, he didn't disappear! He's still under my bed and-" David interrupted, "Well, I'll take a look, and see for myself." As he got on the floor and peered under the bed, something moved that made him jump. He bumped his head on the bed frame. A motion activated, Dino-the-Dinosaur, appeared out from under the bed. "Are you alright?" asked Sandra. "Ouch! I think so," he said, rubbing his head with one hand, and holding Dino with the other, "that really hurt!" Derek was out of his bed in an instant. "It's Dino!" he yelled, with delight, "I wondered what happened to him. I couldn't find him for a long time." David handed the Flintstone's toy to Derek. "That was probably what you two thought you heard under the bed," said Sandra. "But mommy, what about the soldier I saw?" Ruthann asked. "Well, sometimes when we are waking up from a dream, we don't always know at first, if it's real or not. You were probably dreaming of a soldier when the sound woke you up. Derek, you didn't really hear, and see him too did you?" Derek shook his head. "No, mommy. I guess not. Ruthie was just really scaring me with her yelling."

Sandra was glad that the children and David were sound asleep after all the excitement, but she wished she could go back to sleep too. She kept thinking about all the things she had to get done before Derek's birthday party. The clock radio showed that it was five thirty. She decided that she might as well get up and start getting things done, instead of just laying there thinking about it. So much for getting more rest on the weekend.

The living room and kitchen were decorated with balloons and streamers. A poster of pin-the-tail on the donkey was taped to the sliding glass door in the kitchen. The peanut butter cookies were done, and the Dino Dinosaur cake was on the counter with four yellow candles on it. Guests would be arriving soon. Sandra still had to change her clothes and fix her hair. As she was putting the hot rollers in her long brown hair, she realized how tired she was. Just the thought of two hours of entertaining guests was exhausting. She would have to be strong, and act like her high energetic self. It wouldn't take much out of the ordinary for her mother, Maggie, to notice it and be curious.

As Sandra finished taking the last roller out of her hair, she heard the doorbell ring. She could hear the children yelling "Grandma! It's grandma". When Sandra walked into the living room, her mother glanced at her with a smile, as she hugged her grandchildren. "You are getting to be such a big boy Derek," she said, "and you are so pretty in that green dress, Baby Ruth." Ruthann twirled around to make her dress flare out. "Thanks grandma!" she said. Derek stood as straight and tall as he could. "I will be as tall as daddy soon," he said, proudly. "Grandma, green is my favorite color," added Ruthann, who was wanting more attention.

Sandra told the children to hurry, and make sure all the toys were picked up and put away. "Hi mom," she said as she gave her a big hug. Sandra's mother, Maggie, was a sweet, polite, and quiet person. She wore her hair in braids that she wrapped on top of her head. It was an old-fashioned style, but it looked very attractive on her. She dressed plainly, and always wore dresses. The only jewelry that she wore was her wedding band. "It's so good to see you Sandra. Going three weeks without seeing my daughter, when she lives in the very same town, is way too long! I just don't get out much anymore now that your father isn't well," said Maggie, with a sigh. "Mom, I understand, so you don't have to feel guilty about it. I know where you live too, you know." Stepping back a foot, with her hands on Sandra's shoulders, Maggie paused and took a good look at her. "Mom!" Sandra exclaimed. "Do you feel alright? You look tired," Maggie said, with raised eyebrows. Sandra turned around and started toward the kitchen. "I'm fine mother, come on, and help me put the kid's goody bags out at each place on the table."

As they entered the kitchen, David looked up from stirring the Kool-Aid. He greeted his mother-in-law with a hug. "Hello Maggie," he said, greeting his mother-in-law, "how's Evan doing?" She walked over to him and gave him a big hug. "He's doing okay. He's just as ornery as ever though. He is as stubborn as a mule." David laughed. "Now, don't you worry. We'll work on him and wear him down. He'll give in and go to the doctor just to shut us up." David went back to stirring. Maggie smiled at him, and asked what she could do to help out in the kitchen. David always had a way of making her feel better with his encouraging words.

There was a good turnout at the party, with a total of twenty-seven guests. Derek received many nice gifts. He was especially happy to get the Toss-Across game that he had been asking for. The kids had a wonderful time playing games and eating goodies. When the last guest left, Sandra gave a big sigh of relief that no one, not even her mother, suspected anything. At one point, after eating a peanut butter cookie, she thought she was going to be sick. She fought the feeling and recovered. After the kitchen was cleaned up, and the children were put to bed, she fell into bed exhausted, and in no time she was asleep.

CHAPTER *Three*

Give Me Strength

Sandra rolled over on her back and stretched. When she opened her eyes, she was surprised to see that it was daylight. It sure felt good to get a good night's sleep. She gently nudged David. "Honey, it's eight o'clock, and the kids haven't come in to wake us up yet. Now, that doesn't happen very often on the weekends. Listen." David sat up. "Listen to what?" Sandra quickly sat up too. "That's just it," she said, "nothing. It's way too quiet. The kids wouldn't still be asleep. I better go, and see what's going on."

As she walked down the hall, she could hear the children talking. When she entered the kitchen, she stopped in her tracks. With her eyes and mouth wide open, she just stood there for a moment. She couldn't move or speak. She needed a moment to take it all in. She couldn't believe her eyes. There on the kitchen counter, sat Derek and Ruthann, covered head to toe with flour. Something gooey was all over the front of Derek's pajama top, running down the cabinet door, and dripping onto the floor. Ruthann had a large spoon filled with peanut butter, and had it up to her mouth.

They heard her gasp, and turned to see her standing there. When they saw the look on her face, they sat still, with eyes wide as saucers. Sandra couldn't speak. She knew, if she did, she would say something she'd regret. At first she wanted to yell, or cry, and then finally, she decided to laugh instead. She didn't hold back at all. While leaning in the doorway, she covered her face with her hands, and went from laughing to crying. "Mommy!" said Ruthann. "What's wrong?" asked Derek. "I'm okay!" Sandra managed to say. She wiped her eyes on the sleeve of her robe, and walked over to them. She smiled, and asked them what they were doing. "We wanted to surprise you and daddy, and cook you a great big cake for breakfast," said Derek. "That's right mommy," said Ruthann, "all the birthday cake got eaten up yesterday." Ruthann licked the spoon of peanut butter she was holding. "Where did you get your recipe?" asked Sandra, sniffling. "We made it up ourselves," said Derek, looking very proud of himself.

David walked into the kitchen. He knew right away that Sandra could not be feeling happy about the situation. He walked over to Sandra and put his arm around her. "I'll help you finish up here, while mommy takes a shower," said David, enthusiastically, to the children. He whispered to Sandra that she could have the day to herself. She could rest while he took the children fishing for the day. David gently turned her around, and gave her a little push in the other direction. It was times like this that she felt so fortunate to have a husband so thoughtful and loving.

David took the children with him to his favorite place to fish. Ruthann liked to dig holes on the bank of the lake, and put rocks in her bucket. Derek loved fishing, and never wanted to stop until he caught one. A co-worker of David's, Wilber, was there when they arrived. He was a scruffy looking man, sitting on a log, and chewing tobacco. "Hey, Stew," said Wilber, "What a surprise. I didn't know you fished here." David didn't care much for the man, but was kind to him, and reached out to shake his hand. "Well, Wilber, I've been pretty busy the past few months, so my fishing pole has been neglected. Are you catching anything?" asked David. "At first, I caught two catfish, but I got nothing in the last forty-five minutes. Say, that sure is a pretty little thing you got there, and a healthy looking boy too," Wilber said, as he patted Derek's back. Derek staggered a bit from the powerful pat on the back. Wilber glanced towards Ruthann and said, "Hi Sweet Pea." Ruthann didn't hear him. She spotted some interesting looking rocks, and ran toward them.

Derek and Wilber were chatting, while David was giving Ruthann instructions not to get close to the edge of the water. "Your sister sure is a little darling. I'd say she's about the age of my granddaughter," said

Wilber, as he spit out his tobacco. "I just turned 5 yesterday," said Derek, proudly. "That's nice son. What is your sister's name?" Derek kicked a rock into the water. "My name is Derek, and I'll be in kindergarten soon. I like-" Wilber gave him a hard pat on the back again. "Look kid, I didn't ask about you. I asked what your sister's name is. Are you going to tell me, or not?" David and Ruthann made their way farther down the bank. David was busy baiting two fishing poles and Ruthann was playing with rocks. David would have been angry, if he heard the rude way Wilber was talking to Derek. "Sure, I'll tell you," Derek said, with a hurt look on his face, "her name is Ruthann. Grandma calls her Baby Ruth, but I call her Ruthie. Some people-" Wilber didn't have any patience for Derek, and interrupted him again. "Okay, kid. I think I've got it. Now scoot!" Derek picked up some rocks, and threw them in the water towards Wilber's fishing line. "Bratt!" Wilber muttered under his breath.

Derek walked to where his father was fishing. When he saw David reeling in a big fish, he started cheering him on, and then ran to get the tackle box for him. Ruthann got bored where she was, and wanted to go back to get her bucket and shovel by Wilber. David walked with her to get them. Wilber and David started talking about David's catch. While they were talking, Ruthann got comfortable in a spot on the ground, and began digging. "Let's go Ruthie Pie. Gather your things. We are going where the fish are," said David, pointing toward Derek. Ruthann didn't even look up. "But daddy, I have a gold mine here, and I need to keep digging. There's lots of treasure here!" Wilber chimed in. "Stew, you can let her stay here with me. I'll keep a close eye on her for you." David didn't see any harm in it, so he let Ruthann stay. He told Wilber to walk her back to him, when she was done playing there.

Wilber could hear David and Derek holler each time they caught a fish, but they couldn't be seen from where he was sitting. Ruthann was humming a little tune, and was in her own little world, when Wilber spoke to her. "Little Ruthie Pie, come over here for a minute." When she didn't respond, he called her again. "Oh, little Ruthie Pie!" Wilber said, louder. Ruthann looked up. "Only my daddy calls me that sometimes. Anyway, I'm very busy right now," she said, and kept playing. "Excuse me, little miss! Oh well, you probably don't want to see my shiny new pocket watch with carving of animals on it anyway." With that, she was up in an instant, and ran over to him. She held out her hand to see it. "I bet it's very pretty!" Wilber gave her a big smile, showing several brown teeth, and a tooth missing in the front. "It certainly is very pretty. If you sit on my lap, I can show it to you better." She jumped up on his lap with enthusiasm, and held out her hand. Wilber took the pocket watch out of his pocket and handed it to her. "This is so shiny!" Ruthann exclaimed, with joy. She looked at the front which had a pheasant engraved on it, and then turned it over. There was writing on it, and a heart engraved under that. "What does it say?" Wilber ignored her question, and smoothed out her dress. "This sure is a pretty dress. Oh! My goodness! Such pretty pants, with ruffles too!" Ruthann was proud of them, and they made her feel like a big girl. "I got a whole pack of these from my grandma when I had a three birthday." She smoothed her dress back down. "Is there something inside this?" Ruthann asked, while studying the watch. He showed her how it opened and closed.

While Ruthann was having fun opening and closing the pocket watch, Wilber kissed her on the cheek. She suddenly disliked this man, and jumped down from his lap. "I don't like your pocket watch anymore! I'm going to dig for more treasure!" Ruthann said, with a huff. "The pocket watch, and sitting on my lap, and all, will be our little secret. Okay?" Wilber said, nervously. Ruthann stopped humming to say "okay" and went right back to digging. A little while later, David and Derek returned, and showed Wilber their catch of fish. Wilber already had his fishing pole and tackle box loaded up. He was ready to leave, and said "good bye" in a hurry.

David and Derek loaded the fishing poles, tackle box, and fish into the car. Ruthann climbed in, taking her bucket of rocks with her. On the drive home, Derek and David bragged about their catch. Ruthann felt left out of the conversation and chimed in. "When I was digging for gold, I found some treasures, and Wilber showed me his pretty pocket watch, and he told me my dress and pants were pretty, and kissed me on the cheek, and, so there!" David thought he couldn't have heard her say, what he thought she said. He pulled over quickly, to the side of the road. Derek asked David why he stopped, but Ruthann kept playing with the rocks in her bucket. David cupped her chin in the palm of his hand. "Look at me, Ruthie Pie. Did Wilber do anything else?" Sounding impatient, she answered. "No daddy, but I don't like him very much. He called me Ruthie Pie, and I told him that only you call me that. He showed me his pretty pocket watch too, but it was supposed to be our secret." David sat back hard in his seat. A fire was burning inside of him, and he felt like he was going to explode. The anger he was feeling was evident on his face. Derek was taking it all in, and was a little scared. "Daddy you look really mad. Did Ruthie do something bad?" David didn't answer him, because he felt suddenly nauseous. He quickly opened the door and vomited. Both children looked at him with wide eyes. "Daddy are you okay?" asked Derek. "I'll be alright son. Let's get those fish home, so mom can cook them for supper."

When David was getting out of the car, he told the children to go straight to the bathroom, wash their hands, and then stay in their room until he called them for supper. Sandra instantly knew something was wrong, when she saw David's face. He put the fish in the sink, and turned to her with a serious stare. He was searching for the right words to say. Suddenly he reached for her, and held her close with his head on her shoulder. David began crying so hard that Sandra couldn't understand anything, except when he said "my fault". Sandra was scared because she had never seen him this way before. "Sweetheart, are you okay? I can't understand you. What's wrong?" David felt so guilty for leaving Ruthann alone with Wilber, that he could barely look Sandra in the eye. He finally told her what had happened. She pushed him away, and stepped back in disbelief. "You left her there alone with him! With a stranger?" Sandra asked, with shock in her eyes. "He wasn't a stranger to me. He used to work in my building, and took breaks with all of us guys. He was quiet most of the time, and seemed like an okay guy. Oh! How could I be so stupid! I'm going to kill him! That scumbag! How dare he touch my daughter!" David's fists were clenched and his face was red with anger. "I'm going to get my gun and take care of him right now!" he said, as he turned to leave. Fear gripped Sandra's mind. She grabbed onto him, and begged him not to go. She was angry too, but she didn't want to live her life without David. If he was sent to prison for harming Wilber, the children would be without their father also. She was finally able to calm him down. David and Sandra discussed the situation at length. David found Wilber's name in the phone book and called him. He told Wilber that his actions were unacceptable, and that he considered calling the police. He also told him to count himself lucky, because he wouldn't shoot him today. Wilber stuttered and stammered, promising David that he didn't do anything to hurt Ruthann. Wilber apologized for stepping out of line, and begged David not to come after him. David agreed that he wouldn't, if he never saw his face again. After the telephone conversation with Wilber, David felt much better. Sandra and David had a talk with the children at bedtime about what happened. Derek told them how mean Wilber talked to him. "I don't like that man at all." he said, with an angry look on his face. Ruthann sensed that what she told her daddy was worrying him too much. "Daddy and Mommy, don't look so sad. I'm okay," she said, as she gave them hugs.

CHAPTER Four

The Surprising News

The weekends go by so fast, and here it is Monday already, thought Sandra, as she pulled into the factory parking lot. She was hoping that it would be a good day for her, a day without getting an upset stomach. Her friend Janet met her at the factory gate. They both showed their badges and the guard let them through. "How was your weekend?" Janet asked. She was a very close friend of Sandra's. Her strong accent made it known to all, that she was definitely from the South. She grew up in Kentucky, and loved to share many of her southern recipes with Sandra. She was married, and they had two boys about the same age as Derek and Ruthann. "It was busy but nice and went by way too quickly!" answered Sandra. "I know what you mean. I didn't get half the stuff done that I wanted to. I've started spring cleaning," exclaimed Janet. "Already? You crack me up, Janet. It's not even spring yet," said Sandra. "I knew that would make you laugh Sandra. You look tired. Are you feeling okay?" Sandra gave a sigh and answered, "I'm fine Janet. Like I said, it was a busy weekend. I am a little tired. You were there at the party, and must know how much work it was to prepare for it. David helped, but it still wore me out." Janet nodded in agreement. "I know, it was wonderful, and the kids and I had such a good time. I don't know how you do it!" said Janet. After they had lunch they sat down in their seats at the assembly line. Sandra gave a big sigh and said, "Back to the old grindstone."

The next morning, after a sleepless night, Sandra was tempted to call in sick to work, but she just couldn't do it. She had a perfect work attendance, and didn't want to mess that up. She made it through the morning feeling pretty good, but she was very glad when it was time for lunch. She could finally get up and move around. Janet and Sandra sat in the cafeteria eating their lunch, which consisted of low fat cottage cheese and salads. They were both trying to lose a few pounds before summer so they would look good in their new swimsuits. They would be taking the kids to the town pool almost every weekend. Janet finished her lunch, but Sandra was still picking at her salad, and hadn't touched her cottage cheese. Janet knew something wasn't right with Sandra. She was way too quiet during lunch, and usually finished eating before she did. "Sandra! Oh, my goodness! Why didn't you tell me? You're pregnant, aren't you?" Janet asked, excitedly. Sandra looked up from her food in surprise. "I can't hide anything from you, can I? Yes. I am, and I'm due around Thanksgiving. I haven't told David yet, so keep it to yourself. Please." Janet gave her a shocked look. "Why haven't you told David?" she asked. "I just found out Friday. You know how upset the doctor was with me the last time I was in to see him. He was even more upset with me this time. David will be upset too, because he thinks it's dangerous for me to have any more children. Thanks to Dr. Woods. I wanted to have the weekend to get used to the idea myself, and not stir up any excitement before Derek's birthday party," Sandra explained. "It is dangerous for you Sandra! What were you thinking? I thought you got your tubes tied after you had Ruthann." Sandra nodded. "I know. I was going to, but I just couldn't, Janet. I wanted more children so bad, and I was willing to take the chance that everything would be okay. Please don't judge me. Just be here for me because I'm really going to need your support." Janet reached over and patted her hand. "Oh, sweetie, you know I'm always here for you, and always will be. I'm not judging you. I'm just concerned," said Janet, sincerely, "so when do you plan on telling David?" Sandra thought about it for a moment. "Maybe this evening," she said, with a sigh.

The next day was warm and sunny, so the snow had melted by the time Sandra got off work. She thought she would stop in to see her mom and dad on her way home. Her mother was so glad to see her. Sandra told her that she wanted to see her dad if he was awake. "Yes, he's awake dear, but I'll warn you, he has been in a foul mood all day. He is upset about something he heard on the radio earlier, and keeps talking to himself about it," said Maggie. "Well, do you know what it was about?" asked Sandra. "No. He won't talk to me about it, and mumbling to himself makes no sense to me at all," she said, with her hands on her hips.

Sandra quietly walked into the kitchen. Her father didn't notice her. She stood by the doorway taking in the scene of her father sitting at the little round table. He had a beer in front of him, and a lit cigarette was on the ashtray. He was talking with the radio. They were having a heated discussion about the downsizing of the steel mill in their town. He worked there most of his life and retired from there. He was swearing now, and telling them that they were crooks to take away a man's job, and cause his family to starve. He must have felt her gaze and looked up. His face lit up when he saw her and he smiled. Sandra loved to see her father smile, and it was rare these days. "Don't just stand there. Cat got your tongue? Come over here and give your paw a hug." When they hugged, Sandra could smell the beer on him, but when he kissed her cheek, it meant the world to her. He was very dear to her heart. It made her feel so special that he never failed to give her a kiss, each time she visited. She took a seat across from him, and admired his thick, dark hair. Not many people his age had hair that dark. Her mother's hair was all grey. When Sandra spotted a couple of greys in her own hair, she was horrified and pulled them out. The feeling of regret soon followed, when a friend told her that pulling them out would cause double the amount pulled, to grow back in their place.

While she fanned the smoke away, Sandra thought about how bad it was to breathe it. She didn't want to be rude, but she promised Dr. Woods that she wouldn't smoke, and being around it was probably just as bad. She saw the annoyance in her father's face, when she was fanning his cigarette smoke away. She cleared her throat. "How are you doing, dad?" He put the cigarette out before answering. "I'm doing just fine except for this nagging ulcer in my gut. Hey, I heard on the radio that the steel mill will be downsizing. It's just not right!" he said, slamming his fist on the table. "I'm sorry to hear about that dad," she said, with sincerity. "Well, how are the kids doing, Sandra?" he asked, as he lit another cigarette. "They're doing great, dad. We all really missed you at Derek's party, but we understood why you weren't there. Please, dad, just stay well, and slow down on the smoking and the beer. We want you around for a long time." Sandra reached out and touched his hand. He pushed the can of beer aside with his other hand, and leaned forward. "I know, Sandra. I need to slow down. It's just that it helps me forget the pain. Don't you worry! I plan on being around to see my grandkids grow up." They both smiled and Sandra got up to leave. "I have to go for now, dad. I just wanted to stop by on my way home from work to see you. I'll bring the kids by soon. I love you dad!" Her father stood halfway up, and then he sat back down. "I love you too," he said.

Her mother was crocheting, when Sandra walked into the family room. She stopped crocheting and smiled at her. "Mom sure does light up a room with her smile", thought Sandra. "Bye mom. I love you," she said, bending over to kiss her mother's cheek. The sun was setting, and it was getting colder. "I sure am looking forward to spring," thought Sandra, as she walked out to the car.

As Sandra drove home, she knew that she had to tell David that she was pregnant, and she had to do it soon. She wondered how she should go about bringing up the subject. What was she so afraid of anyway? He never mentioned that he didn't want more children. He might have some concern for her health, because of what Dr. Woods said. She knew that David wanted them to wait a while before having another child. Surely, he wouldn't be angry with her though. Would he? She decided that she would tell him, after the children were put to bed.

Dinner went smoothly, without any spills or rowdiness from the children. Sandra was glad that the food was agreeable to her stomach, and that she felt fine. After the children were tucked into their beds, Sandra and David sat on the couch and watched the evening news. The news was showing the new baby panda and it's mother at the zoo. Sandra thought it was a perfect time to bring up her news to David. "Awe, the baby panda is so cute! Look how the mother is cuddling with it," said Sandra. "Yes. It is cute," agreed David, "even animals know how to take good care of their own little ones. I can't understand how some parents out there abuse their children! They are the animals!" Sandra smiled, and leaned close to him. "I can't understand that either. Babies are so sweet, cuddly, and precious. It would be nice to have another one. Wouldn't it?" she asked. With raised eyebrows, David answered her. "Well maybe, but not anytime soon. You know what the Doctor said about that."

Sandra's heart sank, when she heard those words. With disappointment, she took a deep breath and quietly responded. "Is seven months too soon?" He could barely hear her, but thought she said something about seven months. He wasn't sure if he actually heard what he thought she said. "What did you say?" David asked, with shock in his voice. "I asked you if seven months is too soon," she answered, speaking louder. "What are you saying? Do you want us to start trying, to have another baby?" David asked, sitting up straight. By this time she had his full attention. Sandra tried not to be impatient with him. "No, David. What I'm saying is, that we are going to have a baby in seven months." His mouth was wide open, and his eyes were full of surprise and confusion.

"You're pregnant! How did that happen, Sandy?" Sandra nodded her head. "Yes, David. I am. How do you think it happened? Come on! I'm sorry that this news upsets you so much, but as you know, it wasn't all my doing!" Tears began to flow down her cheeks. She hoped that he would respond with at least a little joy, or excitement. David sat back, and looked at the ceiling. He was silent for a moment, while letting Sandra's announcement register in his brain. When he looked down, he saw that she was crying. "Oh, sweetheart! I am so sorry!! Please don't cry. I'm not upset with you about it. I was just shocked at first, that's all. A man needs a moment to kind of get used to the idea, doesn't he?" He pulled her into his arms, and her tears became sobs that she could no longer control. David felt bad that he had caused her pain. He gently rubbed his hand over her hair, and tried to console her. "I didn't mean to hurt you with my stupid response, Sandy. Please forgive me. There is a new little life growing inside of you, and that is a wonderful thing. I love you so much. Please look at me. I want to see that you believe me, and that you're alright." She lifted her face away from his shoulder, and sat up to look at him. He wiped the tears from her eyes and kissed her.

CHAPTER Five

Summer Discomfort

Four months went by, and it was time for Sandra's six month check up. The hot and humid, August day made Sandra feel miserable. The sun shone brightly through the window of the examination room, while Sandra patiently waited to be seen by Dr. Woods. As she stared out the window, she thought about the past six month's discomfort she dealt with due to the pregnancy. Because she had a lot of morning sickness, instead of gaining weight, she lost twenty six pounds. The heat of the summer was making things even harder on her. The irritable rash caused from sweating, and the stretch marks itching on her stomach, was almost unbearable. Varicose veins on her legs caused throbbing pain and her ankles were swelling. She was so large, that she looked like she was due any day, but she still had three more months to go. "Hello little mother," said Dr. Woods, as he entered the room. "Little mother?" Sandra replied, "I'm hardly "little" anything these days!" They both laughed at that, and then there was a moment of serious silence from the doctor. He looked up from his chart, and looked at her with concern. "I see here, that you have not put on a pound since I saw you last. Are you still battling with morning sickness?" Sandra answered, with a sigh. "Yes. I am, but it's not as bad as it was. I'm eating a lot of yogurt. It seems to make me feel better. I'm faithfully taking my vitamins also." Sandra left out the detail that she was eating a lot of ice cream. She didn't want to be scolded by him about eating sweets. "Very well then. Continue eating yogurt and other milk products. I don't want to see that you are losing any more weight before you have the baby. Okay, let's take a look at that stomach." Sandra could tell by the look on his face that he was not pleased with what he saw. "It's very obvious that you have been scratching. I'll give you some cream to help with that. I'm concerned about the stretched skin, and how taught the scar is from the last c-section. I am also going to give you a wrap to help support that area. Don't wrap it too tight. I'll have the nurse put it on you to show you how to wear it correctly." Sandra was a little scared that the old scar would stretch too much and tear. She just had to ask him about that. "Dr. Woods, my skin won't just rip open if I get too large, will it?" With a pat on the shoulder, he assured her that it would not rip open, but it might cause mild pain from stretching and bleed a little. "I am instructing you not to lift more than five pounds. You need to rest, and take it easy as much as possible. We will schedule your c-section for November eighteenth, unless something changes. Do you have any other questions?" Sandra did have a question, but she didn't ask him. She noticed last month that the baby was very active, and was kicking a lot. She was sure that the doctor would think she was silly to be worried about a healthy baby being too active. Oh well, she thought, I'll just be thankful that the baby is moving and has a good heartbeat. "No, I don't have any questions at this time," she answered. "Well, don't hesitate to call the office if you think of anything, and I'll see you next month."

While getting dressed, Sandra hated the thought of going back out to the ninety-five degree weather. At least she had the rest of the day off, and didn't have to go back to the hot factory to work on the assembly line of radios. On Sandra's way home she would be driving by Dairy Queen. A cold treat sounded so good to her. She needed to gain weight anyway, and would guiltlessly enjoy every bite of the ice cream sundae that she was going to order.

The house was very quiet when Sandra got home. The children were still at the sitter's, and David was still at the foundry where he worked. She settled down into the recliner, and shut her eyes. In no time, she drifted off to sleep. The sound of the children's laughter woke her up, and she looked at her watch. It was four in the afternoon. She was surprised that she slept until they got home. David tried to quiet the children so that Sandra could rest a while longer. They knew better than to jump on her lap now that her belly was big, and they knew that their mommy was going to have a baby. Derek was such a helpful little boy. He often asked her if she needed a drink, if he could help her sweep the kitchen floor, or dry the dishes. Ruthann wasn't as helpful, but was very curious, and always asking questions. "Hi mommy," said Ruthann, "can I hear the baby today?" Sandra reached for her daughter's hand. "I don't think you can hear the baby, Ruthann, but you can put your hand on my tummy, and you might feel the baby move." Derek stepped up, and said, "I'll be next mommy." Ruthann put her ear up to Sandra's belly and yelled, "I hear it! It's making gurgling sounds." David and Sandra burst into laughter. "I think that's your mommy's tummy growling," said David. "Oh," she said, sounding very disappointed. She put both of her hands on Sandra's belly. "Now, I'm going to feel the baby move." Ruthann closed her eyes for a moment. "I feel it move. I do! I really do!" Derek jumped up and down with excitement. "It's my turn. It's my turn." Ruthann stepped out of the way, and Derek took his turn. "I can feel the baby moving too, mommy! I think he's jumping around in there." Sandra smiled at Derek. "He?" she asked. "Mommy, I've wanted a baby brother so bad, for a long time. I know it's a baby boy." David stood next to Sandra, and bent down to give her a kiss. "We will soon find out if it is a girl or boy, and we will take whatever we get, right Sweetheart?" he said, lovingly. Sandra smiled. "Right!" She put his hand on her belly and said, "now it's daddy's turn to feel the baby move." David put his other hand on her too, and rolled his eyes back and forth. "Humm. The baby is jumping around in there," said David, looking at Derek, "perhaps it is a little boy." Derek's face lit up with a smile.

Ruthann was no longer interested in the movement of the baby, and she wanted to go outside and play. Sandra told the children they could go play until supper was ready. They rushed out of the kitchen sliding door, to the backyard. They immediately ran to their new swing set. For a minute or two David watched the children play, and it warmed his heart to see their happiness. He was so glad they were strong and healthy, and he hoped that the new baby would be healthy too. Attending church was never important to him, and he could only remember praying a couple of times in his life; but at that very moment in the kitchen, he silently asked God to protect the baby and let it be healthy.

Sandra was peeling potatoes when David walked over to her, and wrapped his arms around her. "It will be nice when you can reach all the way around me again, won't it?" asked Sandra. "Oh, I don't know. I have more of you to love right now, and I can hold two people at once. You know that our son is going to be disappointed if he doesn't get a baby brother, but our daughter doesn't seem to care either way." Sandra poured herself a glass of water. "I know. I'm not sure how she's going to react when there's a new baby in the house, and she won't be the baby anymore." As Sandra walked past the sliding door, she looked outside, and what she saw horrified her. She screamed, dropped the glass of water, and rushed out of the sliding door. "No!" she screamed, as she ran towards the children as fast as she could. David saw what was happening after he heard her scream, and ran past her. He snatched Ruthann away from the fence just in time. The little girl next door dropped a brick over the fence where Ruthann stood seconds ago. Sandra felt faint and fell to her knees. With her head in her hands, she thanked God that Ruthann was safe. Little did she and David know that they both prayed to God that evening.

When Sandra finally looked up, Ruthann was standing by Derek, and David was talking to the neighbor girl. She looked like she was going to cry. She jumped off the bucket that she was standing on, and ran to her house. David walked to where Sandra was kneeling, and helped her up. He looked back at the neighbor girl's house, and just shook his head, and wiped his brow.

"Now that was way too close!" yelled David, "I wonder what in the world got into little Patty to want to do such a thing, and where did she get that brick?" Sandra was holding her hands over her heart. "What did you say to her?" she asked, out of breath. "Well, I wanted to say more than I did, but she ran off. I just asked her why she was going to throw a brick over the fence where Ruthann was standing. I told her that she could have hurt her very bad, and that she should know better than to do something like that. That's when she ran off. I think we should go over there right now and talk to her parents."

Sandra knew that Patty's family was having some problems. Her father was very sick, and her mother was trying to support the family financially on her own. Patty's older brother was a handful for them, and was always getting in trouble at school. "Let's wait David. I don't want to go over there right now, and supper is almost ready. I think we should give Patty a chance to think about what she was doing, and maybe she will tell her mother about it first. We can discuss it with her later, okay? Please?" David didn't like the idea, but he realized that it was what Sandra really thought was right. "Oh, alright honey, but we need to confront her mother with the situation, if she doesn't come to us soon. It's not something that we should sweep under the rug. She could have killed Ruthann. If Patty doesn't realize the seriousness of her actions, she may do something like that again."

Ruthann walked up to them with tears in her eyes. "All I did was tell Patty that our new swing set was fun, and that she can come over sometime to play on it with us. I just wanted to share it with her. I'm not sure why she picked up the brick, but maybe she wanted to throw it at me. I don't think she likes me." Ruthann was sobbing so hard that her little body was shaking. Sandra picked her up. "It's okay sweetie. Don't cry. Sometimes people get jealous because they feel left out or sad. They might do things they really don't mean to, and are sorry for it later. Patty does like you. You have always been nice to her. Now dry your eyes, and let's forget about this for now. We're having meatloaf and fried potatoes for supper." Ruthann wiped her eyes on Sandra's apron strap, and rubbed her nose on it too. "Okay, mommy," she said, "I like meatloaf." Sandra kissed her on the forehead. "I know you do sweetie." She took her by the hand, and led her to her chair at the table.

Sandra was quiet during supper. She was basking in the warmth and joy of her family being around the table together. She loved to hear her family's laughter, and the adoration she saw in her husband's eyes for her and the children. There was so much for her to be thankful for. They had good jobs to provide for their growing family. The dream they had of owning their own home, was finally a reality. In spite of all that, fear and uncertainty gripped her heart at times. Some nights the fear caused her anxiety and lack of sleep. She wished she could be sure that everything would be okay. There was a longing for peace in her soul. Her thoughts went to the moment when she spontaneously thanked

God for the protection of Ruthann. She hadn't considered Him much in the past, but recently God came to her mind quite often. She thought about the baby growing inside of her, and she wanted it to be healthy. Sandra remembered that her other neighbor, Sally, invited her to go to church, and she decided to talk to David about going. Sally told Sandra that Sunday school classes were available for Derek and Ruthann, and that she was sure they would like the teachers.

Because Sandra was brought up in a Catholic home, at first she wasn't sure about the idea of visiting a Baptist church. She knew that the customs and beliefs would be different, but she wondered what would be expected of her if she went? Although the thought of going to church caused her anxiety, she felt an unfamiliar tug and desire in her heart to go. She was searching. There was something missing, and she longed for more meaning in her life. She was impressed with the joy and peace that the Johnson family seemed to have, and how they were always ready to lend a helping hand to those in need. They were such a loving and kind family. They experienced some real hard times in their past, but they told Sandra that it was God who carried them through it all. When Sandra and David moved to the neighborhood, Sally took them a homemade pie and introduced herself. Since then, the Johnson's had them over twice for supper. Derek and Ruthann loved their teenage daughters, Theresa, and Alice. "You are in deep thought," said David, putting his hand on hers. "I was just thinking about how fortunate we are," replied Sandra, with a smile. "Yes. We are, and I am so lucky to have you for my wife. Get some rest dear, and I'll take care of the dishes." Sandra kissed him on the forehead. "I think I'm the lucky one," she replied, with a wink.

Sandra wanted to talk to David about going to church with the Johnson's. She wasn't sure how he would react, but she was hoping he would agree, to at least give it a try. While watching the news, she decided to bring up the subject. She waited until there was a commercial so she could have his full attention. "David, do you remember when I mentioned that Sally invited us to visit their church? I would really like to go see what it's like. I think it would be good for the children to hear Bible stories and learn the children's songs. Ruthann was very excited when she heard Sally telling me about the Sunday school classes."

David was silent for a moment. Sandra knew he was thinking about the situation, so she didn't rush him. "Well, you know it will be different from the church you grew up in, Sandra. I'm not sure what you are looking for, but it may not be something you will be comfortable with once you go. I'll go with you if you want to give it a try, but I don't think there will be anything in it for me." Sandra looked up in surprise. "What do you mean by that?" David looked at his hands and was quiet again. Finally, he looked up at her and replied. "I just think that a lot of people at churches are do-gooders with a good past, good jobs, and good- Well, everything. I am not going to pretend that I grew up in a wonderful loving home. I grew up very poor. My father didn't live with us or help us out in any way. I have done things I'm not proud of, and I have a hard-working job that will never make me rich. I don't want anyone looking down their nose at me because they think they're better than I am. I had enough of that at school when I was growing up!"

Sandra was shocked that he felt that way about people who attend church. She knew that David, his brother, and sister had a very difficult childhood, but she never saw the pain in his eyes from it, until now. His mother had to take care of them on her own, and they had to do without a lot of things. When David was in junior high, his art teacher saw that he had an extraordinary talent and great potential. She wanted to involve him in a special art project in their town. The teacher needed a parent's signature for permission, and a few dollars for art supplies, to get him set up for it. His mother didn't have the money to help him, and his father didn't show any interest when David told him about it, so he never got the opportunity to advance his talent. The same thing happened when he tried out for sports, so without any support or encouragement, he gave up on school. Sandra and David met when they were teenagers, and they were inseparable. In spite of the many hardships that David had, he came out of it all okay. Sandra loved him and saw the kindness in his heart. She wasn't ashamed of the jobs they had now, and she didn't care what other people might think. She sat up straight and put her hand on his shoulder. "David, you are wrong about church people having everything good. They go through hard times, and have bad things happen to them too. They just seem to have peace through those hard times, and a joy that I don't quite understand, when going through them. Maybe it's because they have God to carry the load for them, instead of carrying it alone. I wish you wouldn't be so hard on yourself. I think you judge yourself much more than anyone else would. You are a wonderful person, a loving husband and father, and you have many wonderful talents. I love you so much!" David stood up, took her hand in his, and pulled her to him. "Okay, don't get so excited. I said I would go. Let's go this weekend if you want. I just need to get a new pair of dress pants if I'm going to go." That made Sandra smile. She always admired how David always liked to look his best. He cared very much about his appearance. She didn't really have a nice maternity dress to wear, but she decided that her good slacks and a white blouse would do just fine.

CHAPTER *Six*

Message Heard

Sandra sleepily reached for the phone, while wondering who would be calling so early on a Saturday morning. "Hello," she said, and cleared her throat. She sat up straight in bed, when she heard the upset voice of her mother, Maggie. "Mom, please slow down so I can understand you. Yes. I just woke up. It's okay though." Maggie took a deep breath and talked slowly. "Sandra, what a night we've had here! Everything was quiet until about three a.m. in the morning. I woke up when I heard your father talking in his sleep; at least I thought that was what he was doing. Well, you remember how your father and his twin brother, Devin, seemed to hold conversations like they were in the same room together, but they were miles apart, right? Anyway, I got up and went to his room, and I listened to what he was saying. It was plain as day. He was talking to Devin. He was answering Devin, and then Devin would answer him. It was so incredible. I wouldn't believe it all, if I didn't hear it myself. Evan was telling Devin that he loved him too, and he agreed that they had some very good times together. Evan told him that he would be okay because I'm here for him. He told Devin not to cry. Evan was quiet for a moment and then said "yes, I believe there is a God. Maggie talks to him every day. That's how I know. You will be okay too, Devin. Just stay here, don't go! Don't leave me! Devin!" Maggie stopped recounting their conversation for a moment, to take a deep breath. "Evan was crying, and screaming Devin's name. I ran over to his side, and shook him. He opened his eyes and sat up. He kept

32

crying, and I couldn't calm him down. I told him that Devin was just fine, but he kept telling me, "no, Devin died. He's gone!" I sat with him until he fell back to sleep at five a.m. I tried to go back to sleep myself, but couldn't. I figured that I might as well get up. I decided to call Devin's caregiver to see how Devin was doing, so I could assure Evan when he gets up, that his brother is fine. I made the call at seven a.m., and as soon as she answered, I knew something was wrong. She was sniffling as she told me that Devin was gone, and that he died around three a.m. that morning. That's what time she was awakened by him talking in his sleep, and he was having a conversation with Evan. I couldn't believe what I was hearing, and could barely speak after that. I always thought he was make-believing that he was talking to Devin. Sandra, it was so unbelievable, until now!"

Sandra was in awe of what she just heard, and couldn't respond for a moment herself. She wondered if it could be true, and she decided that it must be. "Sandra, are you there?" Sandra shook her head and finally replied. "Mom, I don't know what to say. I can't imagine how upset you must have been while that was happening. It just sounds so unreal, but amazing! Then Dad actually was talking to Devin right before he died. Oh my! I feel so bad for dad. How are you going to tell him?" Maggie gave a big sigh. "I think he already knows, if he remembers everything about this morning. He's still sleeping. Oh, wait. I think I hear him now. I'll call you later dear." Sandra wished she could be there for her father at that very moment. "Okay, mom," Sandra replied, "and let me know later how he's doing."

David got out of bed. "What was that all about?" Sandra told David the whole story. "Now, that is bazaar! What a coincidence. I feel sorry for your father. I know that him and his identical twin brother were very close." While she was putting on her robe, Sandra responded with a little irritation in her voice. "A coincidence! David, were you really listening to everything I was saying? They were both talking to each other at the exact same time, and he died around three a.m., when dad was crying and screaming out his name. All those years when everyone was thinking dad and Devin were just a little off their rocker, they were really communicating from miles away. They could hear each other's thoughts. I've heard about identical twins being able to feel each other's pain, and that some could communicate from miles away, but I never really believed it until now. David, Devin asked dad if he believed in God. He was worried about his final destination right before he died. Why do people wait until the last minute, when they are dying or when they are very sick, before they get things right with their Maker? If they believed there was a Maker. It seems to me that it's a little too late by then." David sat down on the side of the bed, and took her hand in his. "I've often wondered the same thing myself, Sandra. To be honest with you, I have thought about where I would go if I died. I believe there is a God. I would like to believe there is a heaven also, but I hate the thought of anyone going to hell. I guess, if we go to church tomorrow, maybe some of our questions will be answered. Are you okay sweetheart?" Sandra nodded and stood up. "Yes. I am, but I'm worried about dad. I'll give him a little time, and call him tomorrow."

It was early Sunday morning, when Derek and Ruthann ran into their parent's bedroom. "Mommy and daddy get up! We need to get ready for church," cried Ruthann, as she jumped up on the bed. Sandra rolled over and looked at the clock. "We have plenty of time, sweetie. It's only six in the morning. Go watch cartoons until I have breakfast ready." The children would stay occupied and out of trouble if they were entertained by Bugs Bunny or the Flintstones. It would also give her some time to get ready.

They were all finally in the car, and were headed to the Baptist church. Sandra was wondering what it would be like. Last week she asked her neighbor, Sally, if she should wear a scarf on her head. When she was a child attending the Catholic Church, her mother made her wear one. All of the women wore hats or scarves in the Catholic church back then. Sally told her that they didn't wear hats or scarves as a tradition or belief, at the Baptist church where she attended.

When they walked into church, Sandra was very surprised that people were talking and laughing. They were walking in every direction to greet people they knew. When she used to walk through the big door of the Catholic Church, it was silent. Back then, after entering the building, people were expected to be very quiet and reverent. After touching the holy water in the entrance, and hand signing the Father, Son, and Holy Ghost, they quietly took their seats.

Sally arrived at church early to make sure that she would be there to greet the Stewart family when they arrived. She introduced them to the children's Sunday school teacher and helper. Sandra liked their cheerful and friendly personalities, and she was very relieved that Derek and Ruthann seemed comfortable with the class. When they got to the entrance of the sanctuary people were still greeting and holding conversations with each other in the pews. It was a bit unnerving to Sandra because when she went to a Catholic church as a child she had to be very quiet when entering the church. Before David and Sandra sat down, several people greeted them with a handshake. A polite young man welcomed them, and handed each of them a bulletin.

They sat in a pew halfway up the middle aisle with Sally and her family. The organist began to play, and then everyone stopped talking. Sandra noticed that David was looking around and checking things out. She was almost sure that he never went to a church before. David mentioned that his mother went to church when she was growing up and that her father was a preacher. Knowing that made Sandra wonder why David's mother never took him to church.

The song leader began leading them in a hymn from the hymnals. Although David didn't know the song, by the time they got to the second verse, he was singing right along with the congregation. He was a good singer, and often sang funny songs around the house that made them all laugh. Sandra couldn't sing very well and she knew it, so she just listened to the words. "What a day that will be when my Jesus I shall see, when I look upon His face, the one who saved me by His grace. When He takes me by the hand and leads me through the Promised Land. What a day, glorious day that will be." She wondered about the part "saved by His grace".

They sang another song, and then the pastor walked up to the podium. There was a burgundy curtain behind him, and a large wooden cross on the wall above the curtain. The pastor began by welcoming all those who were visiting, and asked them to fill out a visitor's card. The cards were in a slot box on the back of each pew, next to the hymnals. David picked one up and handed it to Sandra to fill out. They put it in the offering basket when it came around. The pastor said a prayer, and then began his sermon. The sermon title in the bulletin was "Where will you spend eternity?" The scripture verse next to it was John 3:16. Before Sandra knew it, the sermon had ended. She wanted to hear more, and didn't want him to stop talking. What he spoke about in his message was very interesting to her.

The song leader stepped forward. First he announced that they were going to sing an invitation song. He told them that if they wanted to repent of their sins and accept Jesus' gift of salvation, to go forward. Not long after the singing began, a young man walked forward and was met by the pastor. They knelt there and prayed. As Sandra watched, she gripped the pew so tightly that her knuckles turned white. She hoped that David didn't notice that she was nervous. When she glanced at him, it was a relief to see that he was engrossed in singing. As the singing continued, she thought about how she wanted the gift of eternal life and she knew she was a sinner in need of a savior, but she couldn't quite get herself to let go of the pew. She was afraid! The people there were strangers, and they would be watching her. What would David do? What would her mother think? Her mother took all of her children to the Catholic church when they were growing up.

Sandra wasn't sure if she was ready to take such a big step at the present time. After all, it was the first time she heard the salvation message and maybe she should check into it more herself, she thought. What would be expected of her anyway? The questions in her head were too much for her, and she decided to stay put. She looked at David again as they were singing the last verse of the song. It amazed her that he was smiling, and how comfortable he was with singing the hymns. He looked like he had attended church all his life. Wasn't he feeling the things she felt? He didn't seem nervous or uneasy. "I'm glad he's enjoying himself," she thought.

When the singing ended and they were dismissed, people began talking again. They were even louder than they were before the service. Some were giving hugs and laughing. A lady in the pew behind her was sharing a recipe with another lady. There was a lot of socializing in church. That didn't happen inside the Catholic church she attended, and when church was over everyone left silently. They talked outside if they saw friends they wanted to visit with.

The pastor stood at the entrance of the sanctuary, and he shook hands with people as they walked out. That made Sandra a little uneasy. She wondered what she should say to him. David stepped up to him first and introduced himself. "I'm David Stewart," he said, as he reached out to shake the pastor's hand, "nice to meet you Father." Sandra was so embarrassed when she heard David call the Baptist preacher "Father." She would have to tell him later that "Father" is how a Catholic priest would be addressed. The pastor smiled and said, "Hello, my name is John Larson. It's so nice to have you with us today." Sandra shook his hand. "Thank you. My name is Sandra Stewart." He asked them where they lived, and told them that he hoped they would come back, and worship the Lord with them again. Several people introduced themselves and said they hoped to see them again.

When they got to the classroom where their children were, Derek ran up to them with wide-eyed excitement. "Look Dad! I colored this picture of a shepherd boy, and his name is the same as yours. See his slingshot, and the Giant he killed. The teacher told us a story about him, and how brave he was." David looked at the picture. "Wow! That's really cool. You did a great job coloring inside the lines too. Let's get your coat, and then you can tell me more about it in the car." Ruthann was still at the table coloring and didn't want to leave. Sandra told her that she could finish the coloring page at home, and she could use her favorite magnet to hang it on the refrigerator.

After lunch the children were put down for a nap. Sandra and Derek thought they could use one too, but Sandra couldn't sleep. She kept thinking about the sermon she heard that morning. She knew that she needed to ask God to forgive her of her sins. She believed in Jesus and that he was born from the virgin Mary. She also believed that He died for the world's sins, rose to life three days later, and dwells in heaven with God the Father. She longed for the joy and peace that the pastor talked about, and she certainly wanted the gift of eternal life. David rolled over to hug Sandra, and saw that she was staring at the ceiling. "Penny for your thoughts," he said. "Oh, I just can't sleep. I was thinking about the sermon this morning. "Same here," he replied, "do you want to get saved? I know we need to, according to the "Father," or we won't have eternal life in heaven. In fact, if we don't, we will be in hell for eternity."

Sandra wasn't sure how to answer his question. She wanted eternal life in Heaven of course, but she needed to think about it for a while. She didn't know exactly how to go about it all just yet. With all that was going on in her life, she wondered how she would have time for God. Her job, the children, her father's health, and now the new baby, were things that took up her time and energy. Little did she know that God could take the overwhelmed feeling from her, and give her the strength and peace that she needed.

"I need some time to think it over, David. I want to for sure, eventually, but right now I have so much on my plate. I'm not sure that I can deal with anything new. Do you understand?" David nodded in agreement. "I sure do, sweetheart, and I feel that way myself. I'm glad we're on the same page," he said, as he rubbed her back. "By the way," Sandra said, teasing him, "you don't need to call the preacher "Father." A Baptist preacher is called a pastor." David slapped his forehead. "Oh, great!" he said, as he rolled his eyes, "I insulted the pastor. Oh well. Why don't we stop thinking about things, and get some rest before the kids wake up." Sandra sat up in the bed. "It's no use," she replied, "I'm not sleepy, so I think I should just get up. Now would be a good time to call dad to see how he's doing, while everything is quiet. You know how the children act when we're on the phone. It seems like they are always noisier then, and want our attention."

Sandra felt so bad for her father. He loved his brother very much! They had a hard life when they were growing up. Their mother was sixteen when she gave birth to them, and their grandfather took them from her when they were infants. Their father was twenty-four, and was sent to prison for statutory rape. When he got out of prison, he married their mother, but their grandfather kept them. He took them out of school after third grade, and made them work in the fields every day except Sunday. Late each evening they went into the house for supper, but they weren't allowed to talk. Their grandfather was the only one who put food on their plate, and that is what they had to eat. No more, no less. They knew better than to ask for anymore, or leave anything on their plates. They would be punished harshly if they did either one. Their grandmother was very cold toward them, and never spent time with them. The boys talked to one another when they were upstairs in their room at night. Many of their conversations were about what they were going to do when they grew up, and where they were going to travel. Sandra's father told her that they loved school and wanted to learn more. It broke her heart when she heard that. What was even more shocking to her, was that her father could never remember ever getting a hug, kiss, or any affection from his grandparents. They were very poor, and the grandparents just thought of the boys as farm hands. He said they only had each other. His grandfather wouldn't even allow them to have friends. They didn't have any free time after a long day of working in the fields, even if he would. When Sandra asked her father, why their mother and father never tried to get custody of them, he said that his father was very wealthy and was too busy trying to make his mother happy. They didn't have time to be bothered with them.

"Hello," said Maggie. "Hello mother. I hope I'm not calling you at a bad time. I just wanted to see how dad is doing. Did he remember what happened the other night, and is he okay?" She heard her mother give a big sigh as she replied. "I just put your father to bed. He could barely walk today. I never left his side when he was up and about, just in case his legs gave out on him. He held onto the furniture and walls as he walked to his room. He did remember what happened last night. Off and on all day today, he kept saying "Poor Devin. Poor, poor Devin." He cries a lot too, and it worries me. I just don't know what to do to make it better for him. His heart is broken, and I think he feels scared and alone without Devin. It's like a big part of himself is gone. I try to tell your father that it will be okay, and that I'm here for him but - " Sandra interrupted her. "Mom, you can't worry yourself to death about it. Dad will be okay. I know you will take good care of him as you always have. Do you think it would help if I talked to him right now?" Maggie blew her nose and answered, "I don't think he would want to talk to you about it right now, dear. He doesn't really talk to me about it, other than saying "Poor Devin." Sandra changed the subject, and told her mother how much the children enjoyed Sunday school that morning. Maggie was glad that her grandchildren enjoyed it. She didn't have a problem with them visiting a Baptist church, which was a big relief to Sandra.

CHAPTER Seven

The Arrival

The hot summer days ended, and it was the beginning of the cooler days of fall. Sandra got larger and more uncomfortable as the time passed. She thought for sure that her stomach was stretched to its limit. It was itching and it made her miserable. She was looking forward to the approaching day, when she was scheduled to have the baby. Dr. Woods was not happy with her low weight gain, and how much her stomach was stretching. Sandra told him that she didn't have much of an appetite, and when she did eat, she often got sick. He was surprised that she was as large as she was, with the weight loss she had. He told her that she was most likely going to have a nine or ten pound baby boy.

It was Sandra's last day of work before her pregnancy-leave. Sandra and Janet were working together on the assembly line. Janet thought that Sandra looked like she would pop, if she got a fraction of an inch larger. As they stood to go on their lunch break, Janet was horrified at what she saw on Sandra's shirt. When Sandra noticed that Janet was staring at her stomach, she looked down and saw a spot of blood on her powder-blue maternity shirt. "Are you okay?" asked Janet, with concern. Sandra sighed, "Yes, I'm okay. It looks like my stretch marks are bleeding again." Janet reacted with wide-eyed surprise. "Just stretch marks bleeding again! You say that like it's something normal. When did that start happening?" Sandra put her arm around Janet. "Please calm down. It's no big deal. They have been doing that, off and on, for a week now. I'm just getting so big, that my skin can't take much more stretching. Just a few more days to go! I will be so glad to see the baby." Janet gave a sigh of relief. "You had me scared for a minute! You are really something! I would have taken pregnancy-leave a month ago, if I was you, and here you are still slaving away on the assembly line, with just a few days before delivery." Janet wiped the sweat from her brow. "Well, I'm still capable of working, and besides, we really need the money to pay off our house," replied Sandra, "I'll meet you in the cafeteria after I wash this spot off my shirt."

It was the end of October, and the weather was beautiful. As Sandra drove home from work with her window down, she noticed that the leaves on the trees were beginning to turn. The cool Autumn days were her favorite time of the year. Just thinking about the three months she'd have off work, after the baby was born, filled her with excitement. She thought about the quality time she could spend with the new baby, Derek, and Ruthann all day long. David was going to be off work for a week to help out. Sandra was looking forward to her family being together for a whole week. She was sure that Derek and Ruthann would want to be "little helpers" with the new baby, as much as they could. She thought about the quiet time her and David would have, while the children took a nap. "It will be so wonderful," she thought.

The day finally arrived for the scheduled delivery of David and Sandra's third child. They got up early on the chilly and rainy morning. During the night thunder clapped, and strong wind caused a loose gutter to rattle continuously. They barely got a wink of sleep all night. Sandra was anxious about the surgery, and hoped that her incision would heal well afterward. Although things were set up at the house for the new little one, they were aware that there would be a lot of adjusting to things, for them all.

On the drive to the hospital, Sandra and David talked about girl and boy names that they liked. David suggested some strange ones just to get Sandra to relax and laugh. When they arrived at the entrance of the hospital, a nurse greeted them at the door with a wheelchair. From there they rolled her into a temporary waiting room, where she fell asleep while waiting to be meet with the doctor. David sat silently beside her and held her hand. He was glad that she was getting a little nap before the surgery, after the sleepless night that she had.

"Wake up sleeping beauty. How are you feeling this morning, Sandra?" asked Dr. Woods. "I feel like an overblown balloon!" said Sandra, as she puffed out her cheeks. "Well, you will be relieved of that feeling very soon dear. We are going to roll you to the delivery room, and we will do a spinal block like we did on your last cesarean. You will be awake during the surgery, so you will know everything that is going on. I'm going to scrub and suit up, and I'll see you soon in the delivery room." The nurse took over with preparations, and Sandra held tightly to David's hand. "I wish you could stay with me during the delivery David." David smoothed back the hair on her forehead, and told her, he wished he could too. It was unheard of, to allow the father or any other person, other than staff, to be in the delivery room. "I will be waiting for you and the baby when you get out of surgery. Both of you will be just fine. I know it." He gave her a kiss, and then she was rolled into the operating room.

"We are going to lay you on this delivery table, and then the doctor will come in and do the spinal block," said the nurse. Sandra lay there for what seemed like an hour. The weight of the baby was putting painful pressure on her back. "Where is Dr. Woods?" Sandra finally asked. Before the nurse could answer, another nurse walked in. "Just relax Mrs. Stewart. Dr Woods had to go into emergency surgery for another delivery, and will be back as soon as possible." "Oh, please put me back on a bed until he comes back. My back is killing me on this hard delivery table." The nurse apologized, and told Sandra that she couldn't do that, but assured her that the doctor would be there soon.

Finally Dr. Woods returned, and gave Sandra the spinal block. She was so relieved when the pain in her back subsided. "Okay, here we go, Sandra," said Dr.Woods, "we are going to bring that ten pound baby boy into this world." A few moments later Sandra had a feeling of air entering her body. All of a sudden Dr. Woods yelled "what" which for a moment, scared her. "It's a girl, and it's so little!" he said, with shock in his voice. Sandra couldn't believe it either. Her stomach was huge. A few moments later the baby began to cry. "What's this? Oh my! It's another little girl," he shouted. Sandra was sure, she couldn't have heard the doctor correctly. "What did you say?" Sandra replied, with a quivering voice. "You heard me right the first time, Sandra. You have two beautiful baby girls." Sandra heard a slap on the second baby's bottom, and then there were two babies crying. Her thoughts were running wild. "Now it all makes sense," she thought. The almost constant kicking, her overgrown stomach, and the pains in her back, was from being pregnant with twins! She was overwhelmed with joy. When the nurse showed her the babies, she was carrying one in each arm. Sandra couldn't hold back her emotions and began to cry. They were so tiny, and looked so precious. She instantly thanked God for them. The nurse let her hold them briefly, but they had to be put in an incubator right away to help them breathe better. One of them weighed only four pounds-six ounces, and the other weighed five pounds.

David had been pacing the floor for over three hours, and couldn't take it any longer. He wondered what was taking so long. It didn't take that long with the other two deliveries. Why was it taking so long this time? He decided to go to the nurse's station, and ask if they had heard anything. He was worried about the length of time it was taking for someone to let him know that it was over, and that his wife and child were fine. The nurse assured him that everything was okay, and that they would hear some news soon.

Just when David thought he couldn't take another minute of waiting for the news, Dr. Woods stepped into the waiting room. "I think you better sit down David," he said. "Why? What's wrong? Is Sandy okay? The baby?" Dr. Woods put his arm on David's shoulder. "Now just calm down David. All three of them are just fine." David was relieved to finally hear it, and wiped his brow. "Oh thank God!" said David, with a big sigh of relief, "Wait. What did you say? All three of them are just fine. Who? I mean, what three of them? Oh! You mean another lady had a baby too." The doctor tried hard not to laugh. "David I'm talking about your wife and your twin girls. They are doing fine," he said, with laughter that he couldn't hold back any longer. "What? Twins! How in the world! We have two baby girls?" yelled David. Dr. Woods congratulated him, and shook his hand. "Yes you do and they are beautiful, and you can see them soon. Sandra is back in her room resting, so you can see her now. She has been through quite an ordeal, and will need to take it easy for a few weeks. Although the twins seem fine, we need to keep them here for a few extra days. We need to make sure their lungs are strong, and aren't having any trouble breathing. They also need to put on weight and get stronger. They are tiny. One weighs only four pounds-five ounces, and the other one weighs five pounds." David lifted his cap, and scratched his head. He started to walk one way and then the other, trying hard to get over the shock of having two babies instead of one. Dr. Woods stopped David by gently putting his hand on his shoulder. "David everything will be just fine. We will send Sandra home in a few days, and she can get some rest there, while we keep the twins here for a little while longer. The babies are identical twins so they look just alike. We will put color coded bands on their wrists to help everyone tell them apart for feeding, diapering, and other purposes. The extra days we'll have them here will also give you a chance to set the nursery up for two, instead of one baby. You should also plan to have someone come to your home the first couple of weeks to help with the older children, until you get feedings on a schedule and everything organized. The older children won't get as much time and attention from you and Sandra, but they will adjust to that just fine. Just taking care of the twins, will seem overwhelming at first, but you two will adjust in time with that also. Now, go see that beautiful wife of yours."

As David walked through the halls on his way to Sandra's room, he had many thoughts going through his head. Dr. Woods told him that he would have time to set the nursery up for two babies instead of one. What nursery? They didn't even have a nursery set up for one. Their home only had two bedrooms, so the twins would be in their room at first, and then would be moved into Ruthann and Derek's room later. Like the doctor said "everyone will have to adjust", he thought. As David entered Sandra's room, he saw that her eyes were closed. He quietly walked up to Sandra's bed, and thought she was sleeping. He just stood there gazing at her for a few moments. "My Sandy is lovely. I'm the luckiest man in the world," he thought. "I heard you come in, David," she said, as she opened her eyes, "I guess you are as speechless as I was, when I first heard the news." He leaned over and kissed her. He was so excited as he talked about the arrival of the twins, that he could hardly control himself. "I have twins!" he cried, throwing his arms in the air, "I never dreamed that I could have twins. Can you believe it?" Sandra tried to control her laughter, as much as she could, because it hurt so bad when she did. "Oh don't make me laugh, sweetheart! It hurts where my stitches are, if you do. No! I never dreamed that we would have twins," she said, holding her hands over her stomach. "Honey, I can't wait to see them, but I wanted to see you first. Dr. Woods told me how little they weigh. They must be very small," David said, with concern. "Don't worry. They are small, but they are both doing fine. I'm so thankful that they are healthy, David! They are so precious," exclaimed Sandra."

David left Sandra's room after she fell asleep. When he stepped up to the window to view the twins, he saw two babies laying side by side. They were wrapped in pink blankets. He knew immediately that they were his twins. "They are so beautiful," he whispered under his breath, "They are so tiny too! Oh, God. I want to thank you that they are okay!" David stood there for a long time feeling thankful, and admiring his baby girls. "I wonder what we'll name them," he thought. "Maybe, Jan and June," he said, talking out loud to himself, "no, how about, Shelly and Nelly? I don't know! I'll have to give it more thought." David was told by the nurse that he could hold the twins in the morning. He put up a fuss about it, but the nurse won. He was very tired and needed to go home and rest.

When David entered the house, Ruthann and Derek were all over him. They were so excited, and were talking at the same time. He couldn't understand a thing they said. He thanked Sally for watching them all day, and when he tried to pay her, she refused to take it. She was truly a great friend and neighbor. "Hey you two! Come over here and sit on the couch with me, and I'll answer your questions, one at a time." Ruthan jumped up on the couch. "Daddy. Where's mommy and the baby?" she asked, with disappointment. Before David could answer her, Derek blurted out, "Do I have a baby brother now?" The children were sitting on each side of David, and he put his arms around them both. He leaned towards Derek, and patted him on the shoulder. "I'm sorry son. You don't have a new baby brother, but you do have something even more wonderful than that." He could see the disappointment in Derek's eyes. "Your mother is doing just fine, and she will be able to come home in a few days. You don't have a baby brother, or a baby sister." Seeing the confusion in their eyes, he quickly explained. "Your mommy had two little baby girls. That's pretty special, isn't it?" There was silence. "They are so pretty and sweet. I know you will love them!" Derek was hanging his head, and biting his nails in thought. Ruthann leaned her head on David, and began swinging her legs up and down. She wasn't interested in the conversation anymore. He really didn't expect the reactions that he got from the children. Derek looked up. "I guess I don't need a baby brother, because I have a lot of friends to play with down the street." David was proud of him for having a positive attitude about it. "You will have a lot more friends to play with when you go to kindergarten too," said David, giving him a hug.

CHAPTER Eight

Redemption Found

t was Sandra's third day at the hospital, and she was feeling better each day. It would be weeks though, before the large incision would heal completely, and not feel sore. The twins were doing well, but the smallest baby didn't have an appetite like the other one. The doctor said not to worry because she was healthy and it would increase with time.

A young nurse walked into Sandra's room. The nurse's attire was different from the other nurses. Her hair was up in a bun, and she had a small, white, mesh-like bonnet over it. "Good morning." said the nurse, with a smile. "I am here to take your vitals. How are you feeling this morning?" Sandra tried to sit up straight in her bed, but she was struggling. The nurse helped her scoot up farther, and helped her get comfortable. "I'm feeling a little better each day, but I'd really like to try to get up, and take a short walk through the hall if I could." The nurse straightened the blanket, and tucked it in, at the foot of the bed. "I'll check into that. It would probably do you some good, but we need to make sure that you're strong enough first. We don't want you to take a fall."

As the nurse continued taking her vitals, Sandra noticed that she didn't have any makeup on, and she wore a dress, unlike the other nurses who wore scrubs. "How are my sweet babies doing?" Sandra asked, with longing in her voice. The nurse gently took her hand. "They are doing just fine, but they aren't ready to come off the incubators for a while yet. They are beautiful little ones, and the coloring in their skin is improving. I know how you must be longing to hold them close to you. Do you and your husband have any other children?" she asked. "Yes. We do," answered Sandra, "Our son, Derek, is four, and our daughter, Ruthann, is three." The young nurse let go of her hand, and patted her shoulder. "You two are going to have your hands full." She slowly turned to leave, but suddenly stopped, and turned around. Sandra could see that she was nervous, by the way she was wringing her hands, shifting her feet, and looking down. She finally looked up at Sandra, and walked over to the bed. "Would you like some company for a little while before lunchtime? I would like to visit with you, if you do." Sandra thought that was a very kind and thoughtful offer. She got bored laying in the bed all day at the hospital, so she thought that it would be wonderful to have someone to talk to for a while. "Yes. I would like that very much!" The nurse smiled. "Well, you are the last patient on my shift today, so I'll just go clock out, and be right back."

Within a half hour, the nurse entered the room with a bouquet of flowers consisting of yellow and orange mums. "Oh thank you so much. They are beautiful, but you shouldn't have." The nurse sat them on the windowsill. "You are going to be here for a week, so I thought it would be nice for you to have some flowers to look at. I'm guessing that the beautiful bouquet of red and white roses are from your husband." Sandra smiled. "You guessed right. They sure are. He has always been so good about getting me flowers on special occasions, and sometimes just because." The nurse pulled a chair up close to Sandra's bed. "You are a very blessed woman to have a husband who is so thoughtful," she said, as she poured more water into Sandra's cup. "Thank you, I think so too." said Sandra, feeling fortunate. "I'm sorry," said the young nurse, "I haven't properly introduced myself. My name is Rachel Sommers. I live in Bloomdale, which is a very small neighboring town to Westfield. I live there with my parents, my six brothers, and three sisters. I am the eldest." Sandra responded in amazement. "You sure do have a large family!" Rachel nodded with a smile. "I suppose I do. My mother just gave birth to little Amos six months ago at home, and I assisted. The tenth baby comes very quickly, after you have had nine." The realization suddenly hit Sandra, that she would not have any more children, and it was somewhat sobering to her. She had always thought that six of them would be a perfect number to have. She felt a little ashamed to think that way, after just having twins. "God gave you two children at once. What a blessing," Rachel said, as if she knew what Sandra was thinking. "Yes. We feel very blessed, and thank God that they are getting stronger each day." There was a moment of silence. Sandra wanted to ask Rachel some questions that she wasn't sure was polite, or any of her business. Rachel was looking down and looked like she was unsure of what to say too. It was a little awkward for Sandra to be having a personal conversation with the nurse, when she barely knew her.

Rachel looked up and broke the silence. "God is the main reason that I wanted to talk to you. I normally don't share my faith with others, but I felt in my heart that God was telling me to talk to you about His son Jesus. A lot of people say that they believe in God, but they don't know him personally through His Son. God sent his Son, Jesus, to be born of the virgin Mary. Jesus healed the sick, and performed many miracles. He loves us so much that He died on the cross for our sins. He arose from the grave three days later, and now sits at the right hand of God. If we believe, confess our sins, and give our hearts to Him, we will be forgiven. We will be saved, and have everlasting life with Him in Heaven. Salvation is a gift from God, but some do not accept His gift. Some simply won't believe the truth. Others don't want to let Jesus into their hearts because they don't want to give up their selfish and sinful ways. They want to do things their own way, and don't want to give God control. What they don't realize is, that in giving God control, they can receive peace and joy, like nothing else in this world could ever give them. Once we are saved or "born again" as we put it, the Holy Spirit lives within our hearts, and guides and directs us. It's a new life. Jesus living in us! Sandra, would you like to ask Jesus to come into your heart, and live your life for him?"

The things that Rachel explained to Sandra, were the same things she heard the pastor preach about, when she visited the Baptist church. She wanted the forgiveness of her sins, and to have the peace and joy that Jesus gives, but uncertainty was holding her back. There were many questions running through her mind. In what way would she live? She grew up going to a Catholic church and school. She got a taste of the Baptist customs, and how their church service was conducted. It was obvious to her that this young nurse was very different, yet she believed in the same God. What kind of church would she go to? Would David agree with her decision? She was feeling overwhelmed with this life-changing decision that she was considering.

"I'm not going to pressure you, Sandra. Take some time and think about it. I'd like to come back, and visit you again tomorrow if I could," said Rachel, as she picked up her purse to leave. "Thank you that would be nice." said Sandra. "I would like to ask you a couple questions before you go if you don't mind." Rachel nodded. "Are you Amish? I mean, I've seen some of them at stores when I was shopping, but you're dressed a little different." Rachel smiled and gave a little chuckle. "No. I'm not Amish. I'm Mennonite. Some of the differences are that Amish wear plain clothing with no print in the fabric. They don't have electricity in their homes, and don't drive cars. The women wear larger coverings on their head with strings on it. The men are required to have beards after they get married. There are two or more different Mennonite branches that I know of. At our church, the members have electricity and cars. The women in our church only wear dresses, not slacks, but we wear print in our fabric. Our coverings are small and don't have strings on them. The Amish women always wear their hair up in a bun. We wear our hair in a bun most of the time. Amish and Mennonite women never cut their hair. Most of the men in our church have beards, but it is not required. I think I've listed the main differences. I can guess what you are thinking. You are probably wondering which kind of church is doing things the way God prefers. Satan wants you to be in a state of confusion over that, but what the Bible says in John 3:16 is this: "For God so loved the world, that he gave his only begotten Son, that whosoever believeth in him should not perish, but have everlasting life." It doesn't say you have to look a certain way, or dress a certain way to be a child of God. When you become a child of God, the Holy Spirit speaks to you, and convicts you about what is right and what is wrong. I believe there will be many kinds of people and denominations in heaven, as long as they believe in the Lord Jesus Christ, repent of their sins, and give their lives to Him. That's what Jesus wants from us. He wants our love, surrender, dedication, and to share the message of salvation with others, so that they can come to know Him too. Salvation is a gift from God. We don't have to work for it. That's why I have come to talk to you. To tell you about God's marvelous forgiveness, mercy, and grace. Mennonites don't normally go out into the public and witness to others, but they do show God's love by reaching out to people in time of need. I am not afraid to share the message. I believe that God wants me to tell others of His great love for us all."

David walked into the room holding two small teddy bears. One was pink and the other one purple. Sandra introduced Rachel, and they all chatted for a while. Rachel had to be home in time to help her mother fix supper for her family. "It was nice to meet you David," she said with a smile, "I'm looking forward to our visit again tomorrow, Sandra. Goodbye."

David leaned over Sandra, and kissed her. He was still clutching the bears. "What a sweet nurse. I hope you got the rest that you needed today. Hey look what I've got! I have a brilliant idea!" Sandra laughed. "I'm sure you do. How many places did you have to shop to find those?" He set them next to her on the bed. "Well, several actually, but it was worth it," he said with excitement, "The problem of not being able to tell them apart is solved. We won't have to worry about that any longer. We can put a bear in each crib, and keep the same color of bear with the same baby all the time." Sandra tried not to laugh at his idea. "Sweetheart that is a good idea, but what if both babies are out of their crib at the same time for feedings and baths?" David scratched his head while thinking. "We will just have to take the bear with the baby wherever we take them, I suppose." Sandra let loose with laughter. "I think those bears are going to get as much attention as the babies!" David was laughing with her now. "I just wanted to make it easier, to tell them apart. I'm sure we'll figure it out."

David and Sandra talked for quite a while, about Rachel's visit. They were both surprised at her boldness, but thought that it was very loving of her to be so concerned about the life of a stranger. "I want you to know that whatever decision you make is fine with me, dear. I'll even support you, and go to church with you. I'm just asking you, not to push me to make a decision. I may or may not make the same choice. I have enough to worry about, and I don't have time for religion right now." Sandra knew that David was feeling overwhelmed, so she didn't pressure him, but she felt she had to clarify something before ending the conversation. "It's not about religion David. It's about the one and only true God. It's believing in his Son Jesus, and giving our lives to him." David changed the subject. He reminded her that they still needed to give the twins names. After an hour, they finally decided on the name's Marjorie and Miranda. Sandra's evening meal arrived. David told her that he was going to the cafeteria to get a sandwich, and then take a peek at the twins.

Later that evening Sandra thought a lot about what Rachel said to her about Jesus. She knew that she was a sinner, and she desperately wanted to be free from that burden and be forgiven. She drifted off to sleep, while thinking about Jesus and His gift of salvation.

The next day, after she had breakfast, Sandra waited anxiously for Rachel's visit. The morning seemed to go by so extremely slow. Finally, Rachel cheerfully entered the room with a Bible in her hand. Sandra talked about her childhood, and her parents. After a while Rachel opened her Bible, and shared some verses from it with her. "Rachel, I did a lot of thinking last night. I know that I need salvation, and I don't want to put it off any longer. David and I talked it over and he is fine with my decision, but he isn't ready to make that choice yet." Rachel jumped out of her chair in excitement, and took Sandra's hand. "Do you want to go to God in prayer right now, Sandra?" She nodded. "I'm not sure what I should say though." Rachel told her that she could repeat after her, or just talk to the Lord in her own words, because the Lord knows her heart. Sandra decided to pray in her own words, from her heart. They bowed their heads in prayer. "God I have done things my own way all my life, and have made so many mistakes. I haven't cared that you were my creator, or that you sent your son Jesus to the earth to die for my sins, to save me from eternal death. I want to give you my life today, and live for you. Please forgive me of all my sins, and give me the peace and joy that I long for. I need your guidance and direction in my life. I will try my best to obey your commandments in the Bible." Sandra began to weep softly, and after a short pause, she cleared her throat and continued praying. "Thank you Jesus for loving me so much that you died for me. I'm so glad that your blood covers every sin. Thank you for giving me eternal life. Amen." The ladies looked at each other with tear filled eyes, and they hugged. "Oh my goodness, Sandra!" exclaimed Rachel, "I sure can see the salvation glow on your face!" Sandra was smiling. The joy and peace she had longed for, was evident on her face now. "I feel like a heavy weight has been lifted from my shoulders! I can feel the love of Jesus in my heart," said Sandra, as she wiped the tears from her eyes.

Sandra wanted to shout and sing. She felt a joy so powerful, that she thought she would burst. She wanted to tell the whole world, and share the good news. "Oh, if only everyone would have what I have, and feel what I feel inside," she said, with excitement, "Rachel, I want to give Jesus a great big hug!" Rachel laughed. "You just gave Him a lot more than that, just now, Sandra. You gave him your heart! The Holy Spirit lives in your heart now, and He will always be with you everywhere, to help you in any situation in your life." Sandra was so excited, and couldn't wait to tell David the great news. She had so many questions running through her mind. "Rachel what does God want me to do next? How often should I pray? Do I need to buy a Bible? Do I wear different clothes? Should I give up smoking completely, and are there certain foods I should give up?" Sandra asked, with a worried look. "Whoa, slow down, Sandra! To answer your first question, you should pray every day, and anytime of day. You can pray wherever you are and God is always there, and He will hear your prayer. God loves us, and cares about our needs and concerns. He has comforted me in sad times, healed me when I asked for healing. He gave me assurance and strength in times of fear, and protected me from dangers. I thank Him for all that he does for me. His blessings are new every day, and I praise Him for that. Through prayer and reading the Bible, we can communicate with God. He speaks to me often through His Word, the Bible."

It was all so new and wonderful to Sandra. To know that she would never be alone, that God cared about her every need, and that He would never let her down, was such a wonderful surprise to her. "Thank you for sharing the Love of Jesus with me Rachel," said Sandra. "You are welcome, Sandra. There will be times that you will fail God and sin, we all do because only God is perfect. The Holy Spirit will convict you, and reveal to you what is right and wrong. You will know what God requires of you. If you are unsure of something, ask God in prayer, and read His Word. I have found answers in the Bible many times. Sandra, you are a new creation now. You are what we call a "new babe in Christ". The more you read and pray, you will develop a closer relationship with God, and know his will for your life."

Rachel and Sandra had a long conversation about Jesus' gift of salvation. Rachel told Sandra that she would be praying for her, and that David would accept Jesus as his Savior too. They embraced and agreed to keep in touch. After Rachel left, Sanda bowed her head and thanked God for her new friend.

A couple of weeks went by, and the twins Miranda and Marjorie, were healthy and strong. The Stewart family were finally all together under one roof. They just had the first night in their home with the twins, and they barely got a wink of sleep, including Derek and Ruthann . The babies cried a lot and demanded a lot of attention.

It was mid morning when the doorbell rang. Derek ran and jumped on the couch, to look out the window. "It's grandma, and grandpa is with her too!" Ruthann ran to the door, but Derek beat her to it. He swung the door open, and grabbed his grandpa's hand. "Come and see the baby twins! Mom and dad are giving them a bath in the kitchen sink. Grandma hurry. They are almost done." Derek had both of their hands now, and was leading them into the kitchen. Ruthann was still standing at the door looking stunned. "What just happened?" she thought, "That wasn't right!" Her grandparents walked right by her, without a word, a hug, or anything. She could hear them making a fuss over the babies, and they were all laughing and having fun. She felt unimportant and forgotten. Ruthann hid behind the recliner, and decided she would stay there until they left. Tears were running down her cheeks, and her little body was shaking. She sat there for what seemed an eternity, waiting for someone to miss her, and then drifted off to sleep.

She suddenly awoke, when she heard her mother call her name. "Ruthann! Where are you?" Sandra walked through each room looking for her. Ruthann stayed right where she was. She felt hurt and wanted them all to worry about her. She could hear them talking and showing concern. Her grandma was talking about how bad she felt that she hadn't noticed her, and didn't give her a hug, like she usually did. "Well, you should feel bad, and me too Maggie," said her husband,

Evan. "The first thing we've always done when we arrive, is pick her up and smother her with hugs and kisses. That child is used to being the center of attention. Her poor little heart must be broken. I feel just awful!" Derek patted his grandpa's arm to console him. "I'll find her grandpa. It will be alright! I know the places she hides when we play hide and seek." He ran to the bedroom first and looked under the bed, and then in their closet. He ran to the bathroom, and then back to the family room. With his hands on his hips, he looked around the room, and then darted behind the recliner. "Here she is, and her face is all blotchy and red, like when she cries real hard." David pulled the chair out from the wall and Sandra picked her up. "Ruthann, why were you hiding? We were worried about you. Sweetie, take your hands away from your face so I can see you. It's okay." Ruthann took her hands away, and nuzzled her face into her mother's neck. "Mommy nobody acted like they saw me at all. They don't care about me anymore, now that the twins are here." Her tears were flowing once again. Her grandma reached for her, and took her into her arms. She kissed Ruthann softly on the cheek, and told her that she was sorry for overlooking her, and so was her grandpa. They promised that they would never do it again, and assured her that they loved her very much. "You will always be my Baby Ruth, and I love you very much, and always will! I remember when you were a newborn baby, how I would pat you on the head and say, "My little Baby Ruth, with no hair on top." We didn't think you would ever get hair but look how pretty it is now." With that, Ruthann smiled and hugged her grandma's neck. She loved it when her grandma told her that story, and when she called her Baby Ruth.

CHAPTER Nine

A New Way Of Life

wo years went by, and many things had changed a lot during that time, for the Stewart family. David accepted Jesus as his Savior six months after Sandra did. They wanted to attend a church and take the children to Sunday school. At first, they weren't sure what denomination of church they should join. They wanted to learn more about the Lord and grow spiritually. They also wanted to worship and fellowship with other believers. During the time that they prayed for God to make it clear to them where they should go, they read the Bible together every Sunday morning at their kitchen table. Sandra shared their concerns with her Mennonite friend Rachel, who led her to the Lord. Rachel told her that she would talk to her preacher Ezra, about visiting them. Ezra was happy to talk with them, and to answer any questions they might have concerning his church. He invited them to join them for the Sunday morning Service. After their first Sunday visit at River View Mennonite church, David and Sandra knew that it was where God wanted them to be. They joined the Mennonite church, and became Mennonites. It didn't occur to them that it was a very rare thing to become Mennonite, when not born into it. It seemed like most of the members in the church accepted them, so they didn't feel like outsiders. David and Sandra were willing to accept the customs that were required to become members of the church. They became members of the River View Mennonite church, after attending there for two months. The church was a simple white, one story building, with a double door entrance that led to the foyer. The basement held the Sunday school classes, bathrooms, and a small kitchen. David and Sandra felt very blessed to find a home that was only a mile from their church.

They moved into an old farmhouse in the country, eighteen miles away from their former home in Kirksville, and a mile from a small town called Westfield. The only business in Westfield was a gas station that sold penny candy, candy bars, and sodas. On the north side of the building was an auto service shop that had one mechanic to work in it. It was a blessing that they were only a mile from their church and from a gas station.

The Stewart's country home was surrounded by corn fields. It needed to be painted and would soon need a new furnace, but it had a solid frame and foundation. The wrap-around porch was a feature that Sandra liked best. A small well-house was located a couple yards away from the porch on the east side. Beside it was a hand pump spigot. It came in handy when they worked and played outside where they could get a cup of cool well-water without going in the house for it. Everyone used the same metal cup that hung from it.

It was apparent that the laundry room on the west side of the house was sloping a bit downhill, but it served its purpose just fine. Derek got his arm rolled up in the wringer washer when he was playing with it, but other than having bruises and feeling sore for a few days, he came out of the experience okay.

A huge oak tree with a tree swing, and an old outhouse were in the backyard. The outhouse came in handy when they had some extensive work done on the plumbing, soon after they moved in. Sandra scolded Derek several times for scaring the girls, by telling them that there were big spiders in the bottom of the outhouse, that would climb up and bite their bottoms. His teasing caused the twins to wet their pants a few times, and Ruthann would squat and pee behind the well-house.

Across the yard, from the house, was a lane that led to a big barn with a huge double door in the front. A few yards away from it was a little chicken coup. Sandra hated the rooster that ruled the barnyard. It chased her several times; but after it chased Derek's favorite cousin, Mark, she told David that it had to go. Mark was two years younger than his sister Christy and Derek. Christy and Ruthann ran in the house for help when they saw Mark on the ground with the rooster on his back pecking on him. Derek was swatting it with a stick but that didn't stop the rooster. David ran from the garden with a shovel in his hand and knocked the rooster off of Mark. Because of the force that he hit the rooster with, he was sure that it was dead. He picked it up by the feet, threw it in the barn, and shut the door. Sandra ran to pick Mark up. His face was covered with mud and the back of his jacket was torn and had a few spots of blood on it. She cleaned him up and put healing salve on his back. "Do you still want to spend the night Mark, or do you want to go home? I know you had quite a scare but you are fine. The scratches on your back aren't deep." Mark rubbed his eyes. "No. Aunt Sandra. I want to stay. Derek and I haven't had a chance to shoot the slingshot, ride our bikes, or play in the creek down the road yet." His sister, Christy, gave him a hug. "I'm so glad that you're okay brother. Ruthie and I haven't had a chance to swing on the tree swing, paint with her new watercolor set, or help Aunt Sandra make cinnamon rolls yet either." David walked in and was glad to see that everyone was okay and smiling. "That old rooster won't be bothering anyone ever again. Sorry about that buddy," he said, rustling Mark's hair. "What are you going to do with him dad?" asked Derek. "I think he needs to be buried. He'd be too tough to cook and eat. How about you boys come out and help me?" They liked the idea that they could help get rid of the old rooster, that tormented them all, one too many times. They followed David to the barn and he opened the door. To their surprise something jumped out at them. The boys ran but David stood his ground. It was the crazy rooster. It started jumping up and down around him. It flapped its wings and seemed determined to get the best of him. The boys stood back and cheered David on, and enjoyed the fight. David grabbed the same shovel that he hit it with before, and swung at it as hard as he could. His hit threw the rooster several feet away and it lay still once again. David made sure it was dead this time. The tip of the shovel came down on its neck. The boys helped dig the hole for the rooster's burial, and then jumped on their bikes to ride down to the creek. They had frogs to catch and cat tails to pick to use later as swords.

Christy held Derek's favorite duck named Tippie Toes, and Ruthann held her kitten, Tinker Bell. They wrapped them in blankets to pretend they were their babies. The girls carried them around to the backyard. By then the pets were squirming and ready to be let down. After they released the pets, they took turns pushing one another on the tree swing.

CHAPTER Ten

Surprising Transformations

he road to the Stewart's home was gravel, as were most of the roads in their county. Even when the cornfields around them were high, they knew a car was coming down the road, when they saw a cloud of dust moving their way. It took David a while to get used to having a dusty car all of the time. As hard as she tried, Sandra couldn't keep up with the dust in the house. She told David that she could dust every day and still see dust a couple of hours later. David joked with her, and told her not to dust for a few days. That way, she could write notes with her finger on the furniture, for the children.

It was an unusually warm evening for the middle of September, and the children were playing tag in the front yard. Sandra invited Rachel and her husband Kenny over for supper. Rachel and Kenny were newlyweds. They only lived two miles away from them. Sandra and Rachel had become very close friends, and their husbands hit it off real good also. They saw each other weekly, because they attended the same church, and they got together at their homes whenever their busy lives allowed it.

The grownups sat on the porch enjoying each other's company, and watched the children play tag. David cleared his throat and took hold of Sandra's hand. "Rachel, I've never thanked you for reaching out to Sandra, and for leading her to the Lord. It has changed our lives. If you didn't, we may never have come to accept Jesus as our Savior. I want to thank you for praying for me, to give my life to Him too. I know that you and Sandra must have gotten bruised knees, from kneeling on the floor in prayer for me." Rachel's husband Kenny reached over and put a hand on his shoulder. "Hey, I put in quite a few hours doing that too. How do you think I got this hole in the knee of my jeans." They all laughed and then the conversation got serious again. "Ezra told us that we should be baptized, so we set it up for this coming Sunday morning. He explained that he will sprinkle water over our heads. I was glad to hear that we weren't expected to go down to the river this time of year and be dunked in it!" David said, laughing. Sandra was a little embarrassed. "Good grief! What made you think of that David?" He sat up straight, knowing she didn't appreciate his joking about it. "Well, I saw it in a western movie, where they baptized about twenty people like that." Sandra changed the subject by asking what they should wear. Rachel suggested cotton, or anything they didn't mind getting wet.

"Rachel, I want our family to fit in with the Mennonites. You know, to be like everyone else in the church. Most dresses in the stores are short and the girls and I need longer ones. I don't know how to sew, and would pay you whatever you want, if you would make the girls and I some dresses. I need a couple of the hair coverings like you wear too. Ezra said that when a woman gets saved and baptised, she should cover her head with one." Sandra gave a sigh of relief when Rachel said that she would be glad to do that for her, and that it would give her something to do the next couple months, while they waited for their first born baby to arrive. Kenny and Rachel told them what a blessing their family was to them, and the River View Mennonite church. The September evening was getting much cooler, but they stayed on the porch and watched the sun set, as the children played hide and seek.

That night, after the children were bathed and tucked in bed, Sandra and David sat on the couch enjoying their time alone. They agreed that they had a lovely evening with their friends. "We are doing the right thing by conforming to their ways, and becoming members of the church, but I don't think our parents are going to like it," said David, "My mother just bought Ruthann those frilly short dresses and slacks for her to start kindergarten, and you know how your mother likes to dress up the twins. Thank goodness, Derek can wear what he usually does. The Mennonites don't seem to have a strict dress code for men."

He only noticed that they didn't wear shorts in the summer, like he did, and most of the men had beards. Sandra didn't mind the dress code, and decided it was just a modest tradition for the women, but there were times when she thought that gardening would be easier wearing slacks.

"Oh, I almost forgot to tell you. Your mother called when you were doing chores, and she wants to come over tomorrow, so I invited her for lunch after church. They will be here about one O'clock. She said that she wants to see the farm now that we are settled in. You know how she likes to eat dandelion greens, and asked if we had many here." David laughed. "We have more dandelions than grass! We could get rich by selling all that we have in the yard. It will be good to see mom. It's been too long. She's been spending a lot of time with her new boyfriend Greg. I suppose he will be coming with her," said David. Sandra and David liked Greg from the first time they met him. "He's so good to your mom, and he's very good with the children too. They really took to him. Especially Derek," Sandra said, with a smile.

"Back to the topic of conforming to the Mennonite ways; let's not forget about the girl's hair," exclaimed Sandra, "I'm so glad that we let their hair grow. The little girls at church wear their hair in braids. Sarah told me that they don't ever cut the females hair. They believe that it's a sin to cut it. I hope Ruthann will do fine with the transition. That child definitely has a mind of her own. I'll never forget the day I surprised her at preschool. When I walked into her class, and she saw me, she just looked away and kept talking to her classmates. The teacher asked me to stand back with her and listen. Ruthann was standing at the end of a long table, while the other children were sitting at it. Holding up her half colored picture of an apple, she began lecturing them. "Yes, apples are green too, and I just ate one like it yesterday!" With her hands on her hips, she proceeded to tell them that they didn't need to all wait for the red crayons, because some apples are even yellow too! The teacher and I tried not to laugh out loud. I asked her if Ruthann caused problems or interrupted, and she assured me that she didn't. In fact, she welcomed her acts of leadership, and told me that Ruthann was definitely a born leader. Derek is so excited with our new way of life. He loves animals and being in the country." David agreed with Sandra. "I told Derek that he would get a beebee gun on his next birthday. He never misses an opportunity to tell his new friends about it," said David. He scratched his head in thought. "As far as the twins go, they are just toddlers, so the Mennonite ways will be all they've ever known."

After church the next day, David's mother Ethel, and her boyfriend Greg, arrived at one O'clock for lunch. Ethel liked to sparkle and shine. She always stood out in a crowd. She was wearing a rabbit fur coat, a purple sequin shirt, and a hot pink floral skirt. Her high heels matched her shirt, and her long rhinestone earrings were hot pink. Ruthann was amazed at how beautiful her grandma looked. In the past, she always asked to see her jewelry up close, but today she wouldn't. Ruthann couldn't wear jewelry anymore, so she gave her cousin the necklace that her grandma gave her.

While they were all eating lunch, Miranda was chatting away about how her and Marjorie were big girls now, and helped gather eggs every day. Derek Was talking to Greg about his new slingshot and that he would show it to him after lunch. Sandra and David were talking to Ethel about the church service they had that morning, and that they were baptised. David explained to his mother that after a person accepts Jesus as their Savior, the Bible says that they should be baptized. He explained to her that it is an act of obedience. Ruthann was unusually quiet at the meal, taking in all that was being said. Ethel was sitting next to her. Giving a big sigh, Ethel looked at her granddaughter, and studied her for a moment. "My goodness, you sure are quiet today sweetie. You aren't wearing the necklace that I gave you a couple years ago for Christmas. I thought you never took it off. You look a little sad dear. Are you feeling alright?" Ruthann smiled, and put her hand on her grandmother's hand. "Im fine grandma. I hope you don't get mad at me, but I gave my necklace to my cousin, Christy. Im sorry." Ethel looked at her with wide eye surprise. "Why on earth would you do a thing like that?" Ruthann held back tears. She loved her grandmother very much, but her boldness and outspoken ways scared her at times. As her grandmother looked at her so intently, she noticed some things. Her eyelashes looked very long and pretty, and her curly hair had more of a red tint to it than before. Ruthann cleared her throat, and sat up straight. " I can't wear jewelry anymore, grandma. The Mennonites have rules, and that is one of them." Ethel's mouth dropped wide open, and then she looked down at her rings, and twisted one back and forth in thought. "Why in the world, would they make that kind of rule?" she asked, looking up again. David wanted to cut in the conversation, but he let Ruthann answer. "Ezra, our preacher, said that the Bible tells us not to adorn ourselves like that. It is vain. We have to wear long modest dresses too. That's why I can't wear those pretty ones that you bought me. They are too short. Girls aren't allowed to wear slacks either." Ethel got a scowl on her face, and stood up with her hands on her hips. "Well, I never!" David was standing up now too. "Now mother, just calm down and take your seat. We want to help you understand that we are the same family that you know and love. We look different on the outside, but most importantly, we hope that you and everyone notice the difference in the inside of us. Our hearts are changed, and we were "born again" when we got saved. All of our sins are forgiven, and we are made clean. We want to obey the teachings of the Bible, and try to be more like Jesus."

Greg coaxed Ethel into taking her seat. With her chin resting in her hand, she shook her head in disagreement. She looked at Ruthann, and then at Marjorie and Miranda. "You sweet girls will still dance for me like you always have, won't you?" she asked, smiling once again. Miranda jumped up and grabbed Marjorie's hand. In an instant they were dancing around in circles, and singing the song that Ethel taught them. Here we go round the mulberry bush, the mulberry --." Derek stood and yelled. "Stop!" The twins stopped instantly, and everyone looked at him in shock. "Derek!" Sandra said, grabbing his arm, "What's got into you? Look at the twins holding onto each other. You've scared them!" Derek took a bite of his food, and answered very calmly. "Now there's another law for us mom. I heard the older boys talking in the parking lot after church. One of them said that he sure would like to go to the prom with some girl in his class, but he knew his parents wouldn't let him. It wasn't only because they would be dancing, but also because of the songs with music. Music instruments are against their law, and worldly radio songs are too. So I'm sorry that I scared the twins, mom, but they have to know the laws of our church too." Ethel was still shaking her head. " For Crying out loud! You've got to be kidding me!" Greg, who was leaning on the table with his hand over his mouth and trying his best not to laugh, put his other arm around Ethel. "Just calm down sweetheart. Everything's okay. Would you like more water?" Irritated, she pushed his arm away. "No! I don't want more water, but I would like some coffee, if this family is still allowed to have it," she scowled, with sarcasm. "Yes we are allowed to have coffee, mother. Aren't you lucky. It is the Amish, that don't drink coffee," said David, laughing. "Derek, the things that we are supposed to do and not supposed to do, are not called laws or rules. There are guidelines that the church has for us to follow, and there are commandments in the Bible that we should obey," explained David.

Ethel leaned on Greg's shoulder, and rubbed her temple. "I have a terrible headache dear." Greg stood up, and took her hand when she stood. "Thank you so much for the delicious meal Sandra," said Ethel, and kissed her on the head. "Derek, I'll take a rain check on the slingshot lessons," said Greg, patting him on the shoulder. Ethel reached out with both arms. "Come over here and give us hugs." They all ran to give her hugs and kisses. "Goodbye sweetie pies. Grandma loves you bunches!" The children stood on the porch, and waved goodbye until the car was out of sight. "I think all of the changes were a bit too much for mother," David said, laughing. Sandra yawned. "That's putting it lightly! I need a nap!"

CHAPTER *Eleven*

Fitting In

*I*n six months time, after buying their home in the country, the Stewart family looked just like all of the other members in their Mennonite church. They also lived just like any of them, except for the factory jobs that David and Sandra had. Most of the men were carpenters or farmers, and most of the women were homemakers. The people willingly accepted them like one of their own kind, which was a blessing. The Stewart's loved their church family. They were faithful to attend all church meetings, and they were very eager to learn more about the Bible. It was evident that they were growing in their faith, and wanted to please the Lord. The church members admired the excitement that the new members had, and how they desired to tell others about Jesus and His gift of salvation. That was something they were lacking in the Mennonite community. They were not as bold, or as comfortable about telling the world that they were lost and going to hell.

Sandra was admired by the women in their church. Although she had a full time job, she managed to have a garden and can the vegetables too. On top of all that, she made homemade bread, cinnamon rolls, glazed and cream filled donuts, and noodles that she sold to people at the factory. When she made them for bake sales, the Mennonite women bought most of her baked goods before they were put on the tables. Word spread throughout the community of how wonderful her baked goods were. She began taking orders, but she found it hard to keep up with the many requests. Even the Amish ladies in the community were buying her sweet rolls and donuts. Her friend Janet jokingly told her that she should quit her job and open up a bakery. Sandra told her that she dreamed of having her own bakery someday, but that it wouldn't be practical. She had medical insurance and retirement benefits from her job at the factory. That was very important to her, and she didn't want to give it up.

David was very busy also, but he was always willing to lend a helping hand whenever a need arose. He helped Sandra with cooking, cleaning, and even braided the girls hair. He had a lot of mowing and trimming to do. He was putting up a fence to keep a cow or two in, and repairing some roofing on the barn. Soon he would buy some fruit trees so they could have a little orchard by the garden. The children enjoyed helping him feed the animals. The barn yard had a dozen chickens, five ducks, and eight guineas. The children talked him into taking in two stray cats and a dog from the kennel. The dog was a beagle, and his name was Wooder. Wooder was the children's best friend. He followed them when they rode bikes, during their chores, and at play. One of the favorite things they liked to do was play hide and seek in the cornfield next to their property. Wooder was always at their heels barking, and giving away their hiding place, but they didn't mind because he made it easier and more fun.

The twins were growing like weeds. They were talking a mile a minute, but most people found it difficult to understand them. They developed a partial language of their own. Only their immediate family knew what most of their made up words meant. They called each other "Lenny" and "Lonny". Their word for monster or a scary person was "kittyboo". A babysitter was called a "gooshlaw". Ruthann couldn't understand why everyone kept asking her "what did they say," because she clearly understood. They ran their words together and didn't speak plainly, which made it even more difficult to understand them. Sandra was concerned that their speech may be a problem when they start school, so she asked their Pediatrician about it. He assured her that they would grow out of it and be just fine, and that it was common for identical twins to make up their own words. One morning Sandra couldn't find the twins. She looked everywhere in the house except the laundry room. When she walked in there to look for them, they were staring at the dryer with grins on their faces. The dryer was making a

thud sound and she couldn't imagine what was in there. When Sandra opened the door to the dryer, out ran the cat. The twins turned to run out of the room, but Sandra grabbed their arms. "Girls! What have you done? Tinker seems to be okay, but you could have really hurt her." Miranda tried to pull away. "Lonny put Tinker in there cause she got all wet in the rain." Marjorie tried to pull away also. "No Lenny did it." Sandra was trying very hard not to laugh. "Now girls, tell the truth," she said, and let go of her hold on the girls. They looked at each other for just a moment, and then wide eyed, looked back at Sandra. "Kittyboo!" they said, simultaneously with grins.

The Stewarts kept very busy with their new way of living on the farm. They regularly attended church services on Sunday mornings, Sunday nights, and Wednesday nights. When the factory offered Sandra overtime work on Sundays, she turned it down. The pastor preached that it was a sin to work on Sunday, and that it must be kept Holy. Sandra was a very strong believer of the Mennonite ways. She even wore dresses to work, and wore her hair in a bun with the white netted covering on her head. She ignored the snickering and whispers from many of her coworkers. She no longer wore makeup, jewelry, or nail polish. Sandra and David decided they would put their wedding bands in a little box, and keep it in the hutch. They only wanted to keep them for the memory of their wedding day.

Marjorie and Miranda came up with a great idea, for a way to get to know the girls at church. "Mommy, we like playing with babies in the nursery, but we want to have some friends too," said Miranda. "Yes. We have fun playing with the babies. They hardly cry at all when we're there. We want to have friends to play with too," added Marjorie. Sandra was so proud of the way the twins had such a loving and patient way with babies. Their little faces always lit up when they saw one. They spent most of their play time with their baby dolls. They kept busy feeding, bathing, and dressing them. At night they sang to them and rocked them to sleep, as if they were real. It was very evident to Sandra, what gifts God gave to them. "Do you girls have something in mind?" Sandra asked, knowing they did. "We want to have a slumber party here," said Marjorie. "We think it would be fun if you'd show the girls how to make cream filled donuts, and then they could eat them too," Miranda said, glancing at Marjorie for approval. Marjorie nodded excitedly. "I don't know for sure, girls. We just don't have enough room for a lot of guests, and we don't have extra bedding. Having only one bathroom could be a problem too." Ruthann was listening to the conversation from the next room, and decided to help the twins out. "Mom, I could have some girls my age over too. There would be plenty of room if we used our beds and floor space. We could have each girl bring her own sleeping bag and pillow. It would be so fun!" Sandra looked at her three girls with their pleading eyes. "Okay, that sounds like a good idea. Marjorie and Miranda, I'll leave it to you two, to make the invitations with your construction paper and art supplies. Ruthann I will need your help with the house cleaning."

CHAPTER Twelve

The Slumber Party

It was a Friday evening in January, and the ground was covered with snow. There was a lot of excitement in the air at the Stewart home, because it was the evening of the slumber party and their friends would be arriving soon. The twins were talking excitedly about how they could make a snowman, and make snow ice cream with their friends. Derek and Ruthann were moving furniture to make a wide open space for at least a dozen sleeping bags. Sandra was getting things together to make cream filled and glazed donuts. At six O'clock, Paula and her sisters, Charlotte and Dee, were the first to arrive. Paula was a year older than Ruthann, but they were good friends. Ruthann, Paula, and Carla always sat together at church and Sunday school. Charlotte was Derek's age, and Dee was the same age as the twins. Ruthann showed them where to put their things. Derek insisted on helping Charlotte with her sleeping bag. It was very obvious that he had a crush on her, and it made Paula, Dee, and Ruthann laugh.

The other girls arrived by six thirty. Sandra asked the fifteen girls to gather around the kitchen table. She started with Carla and went around the circle to give each girl a chance to help. Some of the girls did better than others. Sandra worked with them measuring ingredients, stirring, flouring the table, kneading the dough, cutting out the donuts, deep frying them, filling them with cream, glazing some, and then spreading the chocolate icing on the top of them.

When the donuts were done, Sandra asked the girls if they wanted to roll the chocolate iced, cream filled donuts in chopped pecans. A cheer of "yes" was heard from most of them. Each girl ate a donut or two and thanked Sandra for teaching them how she made them. They all agreed that the donuts were the biggest and best they ever had. Carla told her that the addition of nuts on top was like having a cherry on top of a hot fudge sundae. It completed it, like a pastry masterpiece. Sandra told the girls that she didn't need help with cleaning up the mess but Charlotte insisted on helping. Sandra was impressed at what a kind and caring young lady she was.

"I'm so full!" said Carla. "I am too!" agreed Ruthann, holding her stomach. "I should have only eaten one, but I wanted to try a cream filled one after I ate a warm glazed one. It was so delicious, and it melted in my mouth!" added Paula. Sandra had to stop Derek from grabbing a third donut. She promised to save a glazed and cream filled donut for David, and she wanted to give a couple of donuts to her mother-in-law Ethel and Greg. When she set the donuts aside for them, she realized that there wasn't one left for her. It didn't really matter to her. She was just glad that there was enough for everyone else, and that the girls had a wonderful time making them and eating them.

Derek told Charlotte that he was going to spend the night with his grandma Ethel. When he said "goodbye" to her, he handed her a note. Charlotte blushed and said "goodbye". The twins and their friend Dee, laughed and teased Charlotte about being Derek's girlfriend. She assured them that they were just friends. Derek was looking forward to spending the night at his grandma Ethel's house. She always had at least three different flavors of icecream for him to choose from and she let him watch television. His cousin Mark would be there too, so it was sure to be a blast. She always let them stay up as late as they wanted.

After they cleaned up the kitchen, Sandra and Charlotte joined the girls in the living room. "Mrs Stewart, I hope you don't mind my asking, but what is that over there that's covered with a sheet?" asked Paula. "Not at all, dear. It's a television that we had, before we joined the church. I covered it because most of the people in the church don't approve of having one. We don't watch it much because we don't approve of a lot of the programs on it, but we allow Derek to watch sports occasionally. We also watch a couple of shows together as a family. There's a show called "The Waltons", and it's our favorite," explained Sandra. "Oh, Mrs. Stewart, could we watch a show tonight? We never watch television unless we see one at the stores," pleaded Carla. The other girls agreed and wanted to watch it too. "Now girls, I can't go against your parents' wishes. The only way I'll allow you to watch a show is if each of you make a call to your parents and get permission. It has to be okay for everyone, understand?" Sandra looked around the room to be sure that all the girls agreed. It turned out that every girl had permission to watch television, and twenty minutes later they were watching "The Waltons." The show had a sad ending, so there were a lot of sniffles heard from the girls. Ruthann couldn't help laughing at her friend Paula who had tears running down her face. "It's okay. Don't cry," said Miranda, handing her a tissue. "It's not real anyway. They're just actors, so he didn't really die," added Marjorie. With that, the older girls joined Ruthann in laughter.

Miranda and Marjorie chose to play the games that they liked most. Sandra led the girls in the game "Simon says". Next they played "who's got the button" and after that they played "twister." Sandra was getting tired, but she promised the girls they could all stay up until midnight. To wind things down, she sat in the middle of the floor to read a couple of stories. She read from a very old book that was published in 1895 called "The Children's Addition Of Touching Incidents And Remarkable Answers To Prayer" by S. B. Shaw. It was her children's favorite book. She chose one of the short stories to read from it, every Friday at bedtime. Although she read through the book at least a dozen times, they never tired of hearing the short stories in it. "Will you please read one more story from the book Mrs. Stewart?" asked Carla. "I'm afraid not, dear. I will loan the book to you, if you'd like to borrow it. It's very late and time for everyone to spread out their sleeping bags and get some sleep." Sandra made sure that all the girls were settled in their sleeping bags, and then she went to bed. She was very exhausted from a long day at work, and a busy but fun evening with fifteen energetic young ladies. It was a joy and blessing to see the girls laugh and have so much fun.

Ruthann, Paula, and Carla stayed awake whispering, and when they were sure that all of the other girls were asleep, they quietly got up and went to the kitchen. "I'm not sleepy at all. What do you want to do, Ruthie?" asked Carla. She thought for a moment, and then answered. "Let's play "Truth or Dare." Paula began the game with a dare. "I dare you and Carla to run around in the snow barefoot for thirty seconds." They took off their socks and ran outside and into the snow. Ruthann stuck out her tongue to catch the snowflakes, as she jumped and twirled around the yard. Carla made a snowball and threw it at Paula, who was watching them from the porch. Paula saw how much fun they were having and joined in. They laughed at one another, as snow accumulated on their hair and eyelashes. After a while Carla got cold, and insisted that they should go back inside. "Now be very quiet when we go inside so we don't wake anyone up," ordered Ruthann.

While drying their feet in the kitchen, Carla dared Ruthann and Paula to put peanut butter between Charlotte's toes, while she was sleeping. She didn't wake up when they put the peanut butter on her toes, and her snoring covered up the sound of their giggling. The three girls went back to their sleeping bags and whispered about school, church, and boys. Paula and Carla told Ruthann that it was the best slumber party ever. She agreed, and told them that they had her little twin sisters to thank for coming up with the wonderful idea.

CHAPTER Thirteen

School Days

It was time for Derek and Ruthann to get enrolled for school. Derek was going into the second grade, and Ruthann was going into the first grade. They were doing well but Sandra noticed a change in Ruthann that concerned her. "David, I've noticed that Ruthann isn't her outgoing and bold self these days. I don't see her wanting to lead anymore. She's more of a follower. Have you noticed the change in her?" David nodded. "Yes I have. I would even describe her now as shy. Remember last week at church, when they had the children go up front to sing. She stood in the back, but I could see her from where I was sitting. She was blushing and I thought she was going to cry. She is lacking the self confidence that used to be so evident." Sandra sat down at the kitchen table and David sat down beside her. "She has had a lot of changes occur in her life in the last couple of years. For one thing, she was used to being the center of attention until the twins came along. Not long after that, we moved and she had to learn the new ways of country living and the ways of the Mennonites. At school she looks different than the other girls and they treat her differently because of it. She used to wear frilly short, store-bought dresses, and now she wears long home-made ones. She can't wear jewelry, and her hair is in braids. She cried the other day when she told me that she was the last to be picked for a team at recess. She said that when the girls jump rope they leave her out. That's my opinion about why she's changed David, but I think we need to have a talk with her soon." David got up and paced across the room and back a couple of times and then stopped behind Sandra. With his hands on her shoulders, he kissed the top of her head. "Now there's one of the reasons I love you so much. You are very in tune with what's going on and so understanding. I admired Ruthann's fearless and spunky personality. I feel like it's our fault that she's lost that," said David with sadness in his voice. Sandra reached up and put her hand on his. "Don't worry. She will get it back, and she will be just fine. She's a lot like her dear father," she said, smiling.

Ruthann was playing outside with her brother and sisters after school, until she suddenly remembered that she had some great news to share about her day. "Mommy, guess what!" Ruthann said, as she ran into the kitchen. "I couldn't possibly guess, but I think it must be good news." Sandra was kneading dough on the kitchen table and touched her daughter on the tip of her nose with her flour covered finger. "Yes it is!" she giggled, as she wiped the flour off, "I made a new friend. She moved here recently, and today was her first day at school. She was sitting all by herself at lunch so I went over and sat by her. She smiled at me. I think she is very pretty. Her name is Marie. She's like me mom. She's different too." Sandra stopped kneading the dough, and told Ruthann to sit down at the table. "What do you mean by different Ruthann?" She thought about her mother's question while drawing a smiley face with her finger on the flour covered table. "You know, mom. We don't wear the same kind of clothes as the other kids and stuff. Marie actually wears her dresses longer than mine, and she can't even wear any print on hers. I asked her about her church. She said that she goes to a Beachy Amish one." Sandra wiped off her hands and sat down beside her. "Ruthann, I've been wanting to talk to you about this very topic. How does it make you feel to be different? I mean, does it make you feel sad or less important than the others?" Ruthann tilted her head in thought. "Sometimes it does. Most of the time I forget that I'm different, but then someone will do something or say something mean to me that reminds me that I am. I hate it when girls look at me and then whisper and giggle. Some even point at me. I know what they are doing and it hurts my feelings. Carla is always nice to me, of course, and Kim is too. Kim dresses so cute, and I don't think she goes to any church at all. I don't know why she's so nice to me," Ruthann exclaimed, crossing her arms. "She's nice to you because you are a kind and wonderful person Ruthann, and don't you forget that," Sandra said, as she stood back up, and hugged her daughter. She went back to kneading the dough and after some silence she said, "They laugh because they are not kind and not thoughtful of others. They poke fun to make themselves look better. Some people feel more important when they attempt to make others look less important. I'm sorry that you go through some challenging times at school, but you must be strong and know that you are very important. You are loved by God and by your family." Ruthann stood to go out to play, while there was still some daylight left. "I love you mom. You always make me feel better when we talk things over. Hey, I'd like to have Marie over to spend the night sometime soon," said Ruthann, excitedly. Sandra gave Ruthann a hug. "I think that would be nice dear. I'd like to meet her. Run along now. I'll be calling all of you children to come inside, in about a half hour."

CHAPTER *Fourteen*

A weekend with Grandma

Ruthann was so excited that it was her turn to spend the night with grandma Maggie. It was a Friday evening, and she didn't have any homework assignments to work on. She had until Sunday afternoon to spend time with her and her grandpa. Their home in Kirksville was a small two story house with a front porch. Beside the porch was a large maple tree with lilies of the valley covering the ground around it. Directly across the street, a person could walk right into the side entrance of the St. Paul Catholic Church. Maggie was a very faithful member of the church. Her friend, Jane, jokingly told Maggie that she envied her because she could walk out of her front door, cross the street, and be inside the church in thirty seconds.

Sandra attended that church and the church's grade school, when she was growing up. Her children liked to hear Sandra tell them stories about her Catholic school days. They especially liked when she told them that the nuns whacked her on the head with a ruler when she talked during class, chewed gum, or fell asleep.

Maggie was so glad to see them and met them at the door with open arms. "My sweet Baby Ruth, you are getting so big. You will be as tall as me soon. Come here Sandra, and give me a hug. You'll always be my sweet baby too." Sandra put the overnight bag down and gave her mother a hug. "I can't stay mother. I have to head back after I say hi to dad. We promised Derek and the twins that we'd make popcorn and play games tonight."

After Sandra left, Ruthann and her grandma watched a game show on television. That was a treat for Ruthann. The Mennonites didn't approve of televisions. David kept theirs when they became Mennonites, but they rarely watched it. He discovered that there was another family in his church that had one also. They only used it for watching basketball games. Derek was a good friend with their oldest son, Lukas. Derek loved going to their home after church on Sunday nights, because they always ate popcorn and icecream while watching a game.

Later in the evening, Maggie and Ruthann climbed the narrow stairway to the guest bedroom. The only furniture in the long one room upstairs, were two twin beds and a big cedar chest. There was a window between each bed. When Ruthann looked out of the window, she could see the big catholic church across the street. She was so glad that the street light shone brightly through the window, because she didn't like the dark. She was also very relieved when Maggie told her that she would sleep upstairs with her, because she was afraid to sleep upstairs alone.

They lay in their beds talking for a while. "Grandma that picture above your bed always makes me feel sorry for the wolf. He looks so lonely and sad sitting at the top of that hill in the moonlight. It looks like he's looking at the town below." Maggie sat up and looked at it. "The picture belonged to my father. I've often wondered what the artist was thinking when he painted it. I certainly agree with you that he looks lonely. The picture above your bed, of the ship and a lighthouse in the distance, was also my father's. It gives me a feeling of hope. Although there are stormy winds and waves, the lighthouse gives the captain light and direction to get ashore safely. That's how life is sometimes. We all go through hard times, but if we keep our eyes on Jesus and the Light of His Word, the Bible, He will give us strength and help us make it through them."

Ruthann sat up and looked at the picture. "It reminds me of a song we sing in church called "Let The Lower Lights Be Burning." It's one of my favorites, but my very favorite song is called "I'll Fly Away". It's Derek's favorite too." Maggie hummed a few notes of Ruthann's favorite song. "I would love to hear you sing the first song that you mentioned, Baby Ruth." Ruthann cleared her throat. "Sure grandma. I think I can remember the words. Let's see. It starts like this. "Brightly beams our Father's mercy from His lighthouse evermore but to us He gives the keeping of the lights along the shore. Let the lower lights be burning. Send a gleam across the waves. Some poor fainting, struggling seaman, you may rescue, you may save. Dark the night of sin has settled. Loud the angry billows roar. Eager eyes are watching, longing for the lights along the shore." Ruthann skipped the chorus, and went on to sing the third verse. "Trim your feeble lamp my brother. Some poor sailor tempest tossed, trying hard to make the harbor, in the darkness maybe lost." Maggie joined her in the chorus. "Grandma, you know that song!" Maggie smiled. "Yes dear. My mother used to sing it. She sang many hymns while she did the laundry, when she cooked, and when she cleaned. You have a beautiful voice like her. She loved Jesus with all her heart. When she was growing up, her family attended a Dunkard Brethren church. My father was raised in a Catholic family. When my parents married, my mother converted over to Catholicism."

Ruthann yawned. "Oh. That's interesting grandma. I wish I could have met them." She didn't understand what Dunkard Brethren or Catholicism meant, but she was getting sleepy, so she didn't ask and lay back down. "The song you just sang has an important message for us, Baby Ruth. When we see others hurting or in need, we should be like God's hands and feet here on earth. Like a light in their darkness, and help them by telling them about how much Jesus loves them." Ruthann sat up. "That's why we sing "This Little Light Of Mine" in Sunday school. I'll say the goodnight prayer that you taught us, okay." She bowed her head and folded her hands. "Now I lay me down to sleep. I pray, the Lord, my soul to keep. Angels watch me through the night, and wake me to the morning light. Amen. Grandma, I like that better than the way a friend of mine says the end of that prayer. She says "If I die before I wake, I pray the Lord my soul to take." I love you grandma. Goodnight." Ruthann gave a big yawn and closed her eyes. "I Love you too, Baby Ruth. Goodnight."

The next day, Ruthann helped Maggie clean out her flower beds in the backyard. She had a big lilac bush in the back corner, two rose bushes up by the house, and morning glories on the fence between her yard and the neighbor. Ruthann's favorite flowers that her grandmother had, were the dainty lilies of the valley. They were spread out like carpet under the big maple tree, on the front side of the house.

In the afternoon they took a walk to the Corner Store. Evan and Maggie didn't have a car so Maggie walked a lot, and enjoyed doing so. When she needed a lot of things, or if she needed to buy clothing or household goods, Sandra would take her shopping. Evan enjoyed giving all of his grandchildren coins to buy candy at the Corner Store. He squeezed his rubber coin case open with one hand, and held a cigarette with the other. "Take as much change as you want to buy some candy at the store, Ruthie. Remind your grandmother to buy me another pack of Pall Mall cigarettes." Ruthann picked a quarter from the coin case. Evan dumped out more change. "You need more than that. Here. Now, give me a kiss, and go buy all the candy you can, and have fun with your grandma."

Later in the day Maggie taught Ruthann how to crochet. She caught on pretty fast, and wanted to make her mother something. Maggie showed her a pair of footies that she made, and asked her if she wanted to make Sandra a pair of them. Ruthann thought that was a great idea and with Maggie's help, she made a pair of them before bedtime.

After they made their way up the stairs to go to bed, Ruthann stopped and looked down at the old cedar chest. "Grandma, may I ask what's in the old chest?" Maggie motioned for her to kneel down with her. Maggie slowly opened the lid. There were doilies, old newspaper clippings, a folded flag, lots of pictures, and a couple of old quilts at the bottom of it. They looked at the pictures, and Maggie explained who the people were. "I love to hear your stories of the good old days. I like to hear about your grandpa whose family lived in Ireland and how they came to America on a big ship. He was proud that he had a family crest and that they were wood craftsmen. I remember you telling me that grandpa Evan's grandfather came here on a ship from Germany with his family. I guess that means that I'm Irish and German," explained Ruthann. Her grandmother chuckled. "Yes dear, you are, but you have ancestors on your father's side of the family too. I think he told me that they were from England." Maggie was holding an envelope and a folded flag on her lap. "What is in the envelope that you're holding grandma?" She took three postcard size papers out of it. "These are called telegrams. Your great Uncle Russel sent them to his wife, your great Aunt Fran, during the second World War. She's my sister. He fought at the Battle of the Bulge during World War II. When he was heading back to America, along with hundreds of other soldiers, he was injured on the deck at their arrival, within sight of the Statue of Liberty. As they approached

the New York harbor, the men began to see the statue through the fog. They were so happy and excited to be home, that they ran to the upper deck to get a better view, and in a matter of minutes they were crammed together. Russel was one of the first on deck so he was standing at the railing. They pushed so hard that it crushed Russel very tightly against it. Although he was badly injured and bleeding internally, he was still alive. He was taken to the hospital in New York City. That's when he sent this first telegram. It was a fast way to get information to people in those days. It is dated February Twentieth 1945 from Western Union, and the message simply states "Arrived in NY. Accident on ship. In hospital." The second one dated the next day, is short also. It says "Please send $5.00." That one is a bit of a mystery. I think he was probably penniless after the war, and may have needed money for the telegrams. The third telegram is heartbreaking. It says "Shipping body by train. Meet at Union Station Indianapolis, Indiana." None of his family had a chance to see him before he died. This folded flag was given to his wife Fran. It only has forty eight stars, because back then there were only forty eight states."

Ruthann looked at the flag and rubbed her hand tenderly across it. "That is so sad, grandma! Great uncle Russel stayed alive through the war, in other countries, but then he got killed accidentally by his own fellow soldiers, in his own country. It must have been God's will to take him home at that time. Ezra said that a person only dies if God allows it. Did he believe in Jesus grandma?" Maggie put the flag back into the cedar chest. "I think so, Baby Ruth. We need to head to bed now. We will be getting up early to go to church in the morning."

The next morning while making breakfast, Maggie hummed the hymn "Amazing Grace." Ruthann sat at the kitchen table chatting with her grandpa Evan. She was telling him about their new rabbits, and how Derek helped her dad make cages for them.

Before they stepped out of the front door to walk across the street to church, Maggie reached into her coat pocket and pulled out a scarf. She handed it to Ruthann. "Women and girls should always cover their heads in church. I hope you don't mind wearing it." Ruthann took it and tied it behind her neck under her long thick hair. "Of course not. I don't mind at all. Our church believes that too, but the girls don't wear a head covering until they get saved and baptized."

They walked into the church's side entrance. There was a table on one side of the entryway that had rows of jar candles on it. Ruthann asked why some of the candles were lit. Maggie told her that people said a prayer for someone when they lit one, or they lit one with a prayer of thanks for an answered prayer. They turned around when they heard someone say "Hello Maggie." It was a long-time friend of hers. She introduced Ruthann to her friend, Hazel, and they talked for a couple minutes about getting together soon for lunch at a new restaurant in town.

Ruthann suddenly smelled something strange. She didn't want to interrupt her grandma's conversation but it smelled like something burning, only worse. She tugged on her grandmother's coat but Maggie ignored her because she didn't want to scold her for interrupting. Her grandma once told her that children interrupting adults, was one of her pet peeves.

A few moments later Maggie smelled it too and turned around to look at Ruthann. She saw her grandma's eyes become wide with fear, and it scared her. Before she knew what was happening she was being swung around, and was being hit on the back, over and over by her grandmother. At that moment, Ruthann regretted that she interrupted by tugging on her grandma's coat.

Hazel cupped her hands, dipping them into the Holy Water bowl, and began throwing the water on Ruthann's head. By this time Ruthann was in tears. "Grandma! I'm sorry! Grandma!" Maggie didn't seem to hear her. She managed to put the fire out of Ruthann's hair, but she ran her hands down the singed locks to be sure. Hazel put her hand on Maggie's Shoulder. "Maggie, it's okay now. The fire is out of her hair." Maggie wouldn't stop. Hazel turned Ruthann around to face her grandmother. "Maggie, look! Ruthann is alright!" yelled Hazel. Maggie saw the tears running down Ruthann's face. She embraced her and began crying too. Ruthann had never seen her grandma cry. "Please don't cry grandma. I'll stop, if you do." They held onto each other and cried a little more. "At first, I thought you were mad at me for interrupting," said Ruthann, wiping her eyes. "My silly Baby Ruth.

I wouldn't slap you on the back for interrupting. Your long hair must have gotten too close to the candles, when we turned around to talk to Hazel. Thank God we noticed in time, and that you still had your coat on. I'm sorry that I ignored your tug on my coat." Maggie wiped a tear from her eye. " That's okay. I should have said "excuse me." You turned around soon enough, and saved my life. I love you grandma," Ruthann said, giving her grandmother another hug. "I love you too, Baby Ruth."

Several people that smelled the burnt hair, gathered around them to see what happened. Hazel told Maggie to go home and she would explain everything to them, and that she would stop by the house later to see how they were doing. She noticed that Maggie had burns from putting the fire out with her bare hands.

Maggie told Evan what happened at the church, and he hugged them both. He noticed that Maggie had her hands behind her back. "Show me your hands Maggie." He gently brought her hands in front of her. "I know you well Maggie. You didn't want us to see, because you didn't want to worry us. I'm going to call Sandra and have her come right away. I know she has those Amish salves for healing burns and things. I want you to know that I am so proud of how brave you were to put out the flame with your bare hands!"

Sandra was at her parents home in twenty minutes with salve, aloe, and bandages. She put the dressings on her mother's burned hands. "Mother, it could have been much worse for Ruthann, if not for your bravery. You need to stop apologizing. It's not your fault. God worked all things out, and protected her from harm. Her hair is singed and will need several inches cut off, but other than that, she is just fine. Look at her in there, laughing with dad."

Evan was joking with Ruthann, to get her to laugh. She was concerned about what people at church would think, when they saw that her hair was cut much shorter. "You'll do anything to get attention, won't you Ruthie? I guess that's one way to get yourself a haircut, but I could think of an easier way, like falling asleep with gum in your mouth and waking up with it all tangled in your hair. You funny girl! Remember when you and your cousin, Mandy, stayed the night here and went to church across the street. You went by yourselves because your grandma wasn't feeling well that morning. You two followed the

Catholic School children up front, and opened your mouths for the priest to put the communion wafer on your tongues. Oh my goodness! I would have loved to see the look on his face when he saw you two girls! I'm sure that he wondered who in the world you were!" Evan was laughing and slamming the table with his hand. Ruthann loved to see her grandpa laugh, so she didn't mind that he thought they were silly. "Yes. I remember. I just thought that we should do it even if we weren't Catholic. The priest did hesitate a bit, but then he smiled. Grandma sure wasn't very happy about it when we told her what we did though." Evan was still laughing. "Whenever you and Mandy get together, there's always going to be something interesting for me to hear about it. I'll never forget the story your mother told us about you and Mandy at her fifth birthday party. She said that after Mandy opened all her gifts, that you girls disappeared while they were getting things ready for cake and ice cream. They called for you two, but you wouldn't come out of hiding. Finally they found you, when they heard you two giggling under the table that had a long tablecloth on it. There you two were, playing with a pile of gifts by yourselves. You two are inseparable, like two peas in a pod." Ruthann began laughing too. "That was silly of us to do that! I miss her so much! It's been probably 6 months since I've seen Mandy." Evan held out his arms. "Come here so I can give you a hug. I'll just have to talk to your grandma about having you both here together again."

CHAPTER Fifteen

Farm Life Fun

It was a Saturday morning, the only morning each week that David and Sandra could sleep in, but on this day it would be an early awakening for them. Derek was the first to wake up, before dawn. He was excited about the baby chicks that David brought home the night before. David put the box of chicks in the laundry room with a heat lamp over them to keep them warm. Derek decided to wake up the girls, so that they could join him, with checking on the little chicks. "Shhhh! Be quiet, or you'll wake up dad and mom." The three girls tiptoed behind him to the laundry room. Derek handed Marjorie and Miranda a chick for each of them. "It's so cute!" they cried, simultaneously. "Hold them tight so you don't drop them, but don't squeeze them too tight. Just pet their heads." As Ruthann held one, she wondered if they missed their mother. "Do you think they will be okay without their mom?" Derek looked at her and rolled his eyes. "Of course they will. They eat chicken feed the day they are born. Their mom could keep them warm with her feathers though. That's why dad hung a light over them for heat." After a few minutes of holding the chicks, Derek had an idea. "Hey, I have a great idea, and it would be lots of fun. I need you girls to help me. What if we took the chicks to mom and dad's room, and put them on their bed to wake them up?" Ruthann looked up at him in surprise. "Derek! They might get mad and ground us, even worse, make us weed the garden." Derek put his arms around the twins.

"You two want to do it, don't you?" They both grinned and nodded. "That's three against one, so we're doing it," said Derek. Ruthann put the chick in the box, and looked at Derek with her hands on her hips. "First you want us to be quiet, and now you want us to wake them up!" Derek laughed. "Yes. It was fun at first, but now this will be more fun. Just wait, and see."

They followed Derek's lead, as he carried the box of chicks. When they got beside their parents bed, each girl took two chicks and put them in the middle of the bed, as Derek had instructed them to do. One chick made its way onto David's chest, and another was up by Sandra's head. The children had their hands over their mouths, trying not to giggle too loud. Two chicks started pecking at Sandra's hair, which really got the twins giggling. Derek motioned them to be quiet, but the chicks were starting to chirp. Sandra turned her head and sighed. By then, there were four chicks on Derek's chest. They all held their breath, as they watched a chick heading towards Sandras neck, and then it pecked her. Derek snatched it up, just as she lifted her arm to scratch the spot. He could hardly contain his laughter. David opened his eyes and saw the children, who were staring at them and laughing. Just then, he heard chirping and looked down at his chest. With wide eyes, he was trying to figure out what was going on. He heard more chirping next to him, and looked at Sandra, who had two chicks on her head. He reached over and grabbed them off her, just before she opened her eyes. She was barely awake and looked around the room. She tried to make sense of waking up to chirping sounds, and why her children were looking at her and laughing hysterically. She looked down at her lap, and there lay a baby chick. She looked over at David who had two in his hands, and four in his lap. David looked back at her, and they stared at each other for a moment. Suddenly, they began laughing just as hard as the children were. In just a matter of seconds, all four children were up on the bed, and the whole family enjoyed cuddling one another with the chicks.

A week had passed since David brought the baby chicks home. They enjoyed them so much that he decided to add another animal to their little farm. Sandra was in the kitchen preparing lunch, when she heard the twins yelling from the porch. "Daddy's home, daddy's home!" Sandra looked out of the kitchen window, and couldn't believe her eyes. "Yay! He has a horse in the car," yelled Marjorie. "No! It's a pony," yelled Miranda. "Oh for crying out loud! What will he think of next?" Sandra said, under her breath. Sandra watched as David drove in a circle around the barnyard. In the back seat of the station wagon, the horse's head stuck out of a window from one side, and its tail was sticking out of the other. "What a sight to see!" she thought, "If only dad could see this!" All of the children were beside the station wagon by the time Sandra got there. They were full of excitement and took turns petting the horse on its nose. "David, the horse might bite the children," said Sandra, as she grabbed the twins by the arm to pull them away from the horse. David had a bridle in one hand, and put his other hand on Sandra's shoulder. "The owner said that she's getting old and is very tame. He gave me a real good price for her. I thought she would make a great pet for the children." Sandra was smiling when she gently pushed his hand away. "You're just trying to butter me up. You told me that you were going to the Amish store to get more chicken feed, and then you came home with a horse in the back seat," she said teasingly. "I did buy chicken feed. It's in the front seat," he said, and then gave her a kiss on the cheek. David put the bridle on the horse and in a matter of minutes the children were enjoying horseback rides, with David using a rope to lead the horse around the barn lot.

After the rides, Derek sat on a stump with his hand on his chin thinking. He was watching the horse nibble on grass. He wondered how old she was, if she would miss the place she was before, and if she would be lonesome in the barn lot by herself. David walked up to him with a pail of water. "What's on your mind son?" he asked. "Well, dad, I was just thinking that maybe we should get another horse to keep her company." David put the pail by the horse, but after she drank some, she tipped it over. "Oh, I'm not sure about that, but I am sure that she needs a water trough for drinking. How would you like to help me build one?" Derek jumped up. "That would be great, dad. Can we start on it today?" David picked up the pail. "I think we better son, or she's going to get real thirsty," David said, laughing.

David heard of an Amish man in their community that sold lumber. He took Derek with him to the Amish store, to ask the store keeper where the man lived. "Go straight down this road for about a mile and turn left. Go down that road, and it will be the second house on the right. You will see goats out in the pasture next to his place," said Ethan Herschberger, the store keeper. "His name is Samuel Miller." David thanked him, and then they made their way down the road. When they arrived, they saw the goats in the pasture. "This must be the right place," said Derek. They purchased the wood they would need, and Samuel gave David instructions and measurements of how to build the water trough. "Mr. Miller, could my dad and I walk to the pasture to see the goats up close?" asked Derek. David gave Derek a look that told him he wasn't pleased with his question. Samuel quickly spoke up. "I was just about to close up the shop. I'd be more than happy to take a walk out there with you myself. I have thirty-six goats including the kids." Samuel saw Derek look up at his father with a confused look on his face. "Baby goats are called kids," he explained. "Oh, okay. I was hoping that you didn't think of your kids as goats," laughed Derek. David noticed that one of the goats was far away from the others and standing alone. "I'm curious about that goat that's alone over there. It looks like it needs to be milked soon too." Samuel looked down, and lightly kicked at a dirt clod. "You are right, David. We will need to milk her today. She birthed two kids last night and they both died. She gives good milk but with the work in the fields, two cows to milk, and the lumber business, we do not have time to milk her every day. Say, would you be interested in buying her? I'd sell her for a good price." David scratched his beard in thought. "Oh, I don't know." Derek tugged at David's shirt. "Awe, come on, dad. Please? Just think. We could have goats milk of our own every day, and mom wouldn't have to buy it from Ethan at the Amish store. You know how mom loves fresh goat's milk." That last statement got him. "Okay, Samuel. How much for the milk goat?" Samuel's face lit up. "Fifty dollars. A special price for you," he said, with a smile. Samuel led the goat into the barn and showed David how to milk her. He also gave him a bag of feed. With Samuel's help, David put the goat in the back seat and headed for home. It made Derek laugh while it kept nibbling on the back of his head. "Dad, it's so tame and friendly. Mom will be so surprised." David turned into their driveway and laughed, as he saw the look on Sandra's face when she saw the goat's head sticking out of the window. "That's what I was afraid of, son."

The next morning at breakfast, David told Sandra that he had to work late, so she and the children would have to milk the goat that evening. "I'm afraid of goats and even if I wasn't, I sure don't know how to milk one," said Sandra, in a panic. "I know how. I'll show you mom," said Derek. "How do you know?" asked Ruthann. "Samuel showed dad and I yesterday. Its a cinch." The twins were getting excited, and wanted to help milk the goats too. "Okay children, I'm sure you can all be of some help. Your father made a platform for the goat to stand on while being milked. We will lead her onto the stand, and give her some grain in a bucket to eat, while milking her. There's a new pail for the milk." Sandra stood up from the breakfast table. "Children, get dressed and brush your teeth. The sitter will be here soon."

That evening at supper, the children decided on a name for the goat. They named her Gabby. After helping their mother with the dishes, they all made their way to the barn. Sandra led Gabby onto the stand, Derek held the rope that was tied to her, Ruthann held the bucket of grain, and Marjorie and Miranda held each side of the milk pail. Sandra began to pull and squeeze the teats, but every time she did, Gabby would squat in the rear and kneel down in the front. "Let's try something different, mom," suggested Derek, "How about Ruthie and I hold each of her back legs up in the air so she can't squat, and the twins hold onto her front legs so she doesn't kneel." With her hands on her hips and about to give up, Sandra thought it was worth a try. They all got into their positions, and they found that it actually worked. Just then Mr. Frederick, the man who sold the Stewart's their house, walked into the barn. He stood in the entrance for a moment, taking in the whole scene that he was witnessing. It was like nothing he'd ever seen before. He leaned on the side of the barn, and laughed so hard that he had tears in his eyes. When they heard him, they froze. Sandra was so embarrassed when she realized who it was. She told the children to put Gabby down. Derek held onto the rope and Ruthann held the milk pail. "What a sight to behold! What were you all doing to that poor thing?" Mr. Frederick asked, still laughing. "Now, just stop that! It did work. Didn't it children?" asked Sandra. They all agreed it did. "Well, Sandra, I just thought I'd stop by to see how you all were doing. I can see by the looks of things, that David isn't here. Tell him to give me a call sometime. I want to talk to him about something. I guess you and the kids have everything under control," he said, with a smirk on his face. "We're not kids. Baby goats are kids," said Derek, with a matter of fact tone in his voice. With that Mr. Frederick left, shaking his head and laughing. "How rude of him to drop by and laugh at us like that," thought Sandra, "He doesn't even have any goats!"

Sandra was still awake that night, when David came to bed. She told him about milking Gabby, and about Mr. Frederick dropping by. He tried not to laugh, but he couldn't help it. He told Sandra not to be too hard on Mr. Frederick. After all it was kind of him to stop by to see how they were doing. He reminded her of what Ezra preached about the previous Sunday. "We must remember the greatest commandment, Sandra dear. Love the Lord your God with all your heart, and with all your soul, and with all your mind, and then to love your neighbor as yourself. I don't think he's a Christian, Sandra. We need to be kind to him, and pray for him too." Sandra was impressed that David remembered and memorized the verse. She told him that she was proud of him. "Well, I figured that I should know the most important commandment by heart, and never forget it," he said, turning to her for a goodnight kiss. "Sweetheart, there's ten commandments. I think we can memorize them all, and the children too. I love you. Good night," said Sandra, sleepily.

CHAPTER Sixteen

Don't Cry Wolf

David and Sandra had to leave for work in the mornings before the children went to school, and the children got home from school before they got home. They needed a babysitter for before and after school, for school days off, and for school summer breaks. They went through two babysitters already, and just had a notice from the current one, that she was quitting. It was difficult to find a sitter that would be interested in watching four children for before and after school care.

Derek was a likeable and sweet young man, but his jokes, pranks, and teasing was a challenge at times for their babysitters in the past. The first one they had couldn't get the children to eat what she prepared for breakfast, which was usually oatmeal. When the children had a day off school, she had to fix lunch also. Miranda was the fussiest eater of them all, but none of them would eat beans of any kind. The babysitter made the children stay at the table until they ate all of the food on their plates. Sandra was puzzled to find vegetables, mostly beans, under the kitchen rug, under the cabinet, and even in the washing machine. She asked the children about it, and they told her that when the sitter left the room, they hid their food so they could get up from the table. She had to let that babysitter go. The next one filled in for a month until another could take over. That babysitter was a high school neighbor girl named Judy. The children loved her. On occasion, she let her younger brother Josh, and sister Jamie come with her. Derek and Josh could really get things stirred up when they put their heads together.

One day after school Josh and Jamie got off the bus with them. Judy took Ruthann, the twins, and Jamie to the backyard to swing. She let the boys go inside to get a snack, and told them to get right back outside when they were done eating. Derek thought it would be funny to scare the girls. He came up with the idea when getting the milk out of the refrigerator, and saw the bottle of catsup. "Hey, Josh, do you want to play a trick on the girls that would scare them? Look what I have," he said, holding up the bottle. "Yes. So what! It's a bottle of catsup. Are you going to chase them and threaten to hit them over the head with it, or what?" Derek opened the lid. "It's not catsup, its blood," he said, as he smeared some on his arm and hand, "Josh, I want you to tell them that I climbed the ladder that dad left out yesterday, and that I fell off the roof. I'll lay on the ground and moan, and you need to pretend to cry. Do you think you can pull it off?" Josh grabbed the bottle and smeared some catsup on Derek's face and hair. "Sure I can, but my sister is going to be real mad when she finds out it's a joke!"

Derek lay on the ground near the ladder, and Josh ran to the backyard screaming. Judy ran faster than all the rest, and when she got to Derek she tried to get him to talk. The twins were holding onto each other and crying. Ruthann was jumping up and down, screaming her brother's name. Josh pulled Jamie to the side and was whispering in her ear. Jamie hit him and put her hands on her hips. Derek just kept moaning. "Derek please wake up! Can you hear me?" Judy kept asking, as she lightly shook his shoulder. She turned around and told Ruthann to call the emergency number that was on the refrigerator. Derek knew then, that it was time to come clean. He scared Judy as he suddenly jumped up, and started licking his arm. "This would taste better with french fries," he said, with a grin. She stood up and slapped him on the back of his head. "What? How could you! And, Josh, you were in on this too!" The boys were leaning onto each other, and laughing so hard, they had tears in their eyes. The twins stopped crying and with their mouths wide open, just stared at them. Ruthann ran up to her brother and hugged him, because she was so glad he was okay. "Derek, you won't think it's so funny when I tell your parents, and when I don't let Josh come over to play anymore," Judy said, angrily.

Judy's second threat is what bothered Derek. He didn't have a brother to hang around with and he only had three friends who were his cousin Mark, his friend Loyd from church, and his neighbor Josh. He didn't get to see them nearly as much as he wanted to. His grin quickly turned into a frown. "Shucks, Judy, I was just clowning around. It was all my idea, not Josh. I'm really sorry. I promise not to scare you like that again. Just, please, let Josh still come over and don't tell mom and dad." Judy stood with her arms folded, but she no longer looked angry. "Derek, have you ever heard of the boy who cried wolf story?" He nodded "yes". "Well, if you keep that kind of thing up, some day it could happen to you. I won't tell your parents, but you will have to sit on the porch alone until your parents get home. I want you to think about what you've done." Derek gave Judy a big hug. "You're swell and the best babysitter ever!" While Judy and the girls went to the back yard to swing again, Josh sneaked onto the porch to talk to Derek. "Hey man, do you remember when we talked my kid brother Dayrl into eating a worm, by telling him it was good and tasted like candy?" Derek stood up and looked in both directions. "Yes. I remember, but you need to get out of here! If Judy sees you here talking to me, she won't let you come over anymore. Now scram, before I clobber you!" Derek said, shaking a clenched fist at Josh. "You crack me up, you know that?" Josh busted out laughing, and ran off.

When David and Sandra got home that day, they noticed that the children were very quiet, and did all of their chores and homework without being told. At the supper table, they took the opportunity to talk to the children about the new babysitter they would have soon. "The family is Amish, and they live differently than us in many ways. They don't have electricity in their home, so there are no lights to turn on. They don't use toasters, blenders, electric fans, or anything that we plug in at our home. They don't have telephones or cars either. They don't have pictures on the walls, or take pictures of themselves," David explained, looking at Sandra to see if he left anything out. The children began asking questions. "Do they use flashlights so they don't have to sit in the dark? I have two of them that I can take over there," said

Derek. "How do they vacuum the carpet then?" asked Ruthann. The twins began to cry. "I don't want to go," said Marjorie. "I'm scared of gooshlaw," said Miranda.

Sandra got up from the table, and walked over to the twins. She hugged them and wiped their tears. "You don't need to be afraid, girls. They are a very nice family. You will especially like the mother, and she will be the one who will be your babysitter. Her name is Esther Miller, and she is a very good cook and gardener. Remember a while back when we drove up a long lane to a house, and you children stayed in the car. I met a lady at the door that I bought homemade butter from. "I remember, and she waved at us," said Derek. "I remember too. She was sort of chubby and had a nice big smile," Ruthann added. "Oh yeah," echoed one twin after the other. Sandra continued telling the children everything she knew about the Miller family. "Esther makes homemade lye soap and quilts too. Esther's husband's name is Adam Miller, and he has a buggy shop. He builds them and sells them to other Amish people. The Amish use their horses to pull them in the buggy to get places, instead of having cars," explained Sandra. David stood while he added some information that he thought was important also. "The Millers have a few cows, but they don't have chickens. They buy their eggs from another Amish family. They have a dog and some barn cats, I think. I know that you girls will want to try to pet them, but they may be afraid of people." David turned to Derek. "Son, I know that you will be curious about the buggy barn that Adam works in, but I don't want you to go to the barn uninvited. The same goes for you girls. Don't go into the horse barn without permission either. You must remember to be respectful of their privacy and personal things. It is their home, not yours. I'm sure they will have many fun things there for you to do though. Just ask permission first, to do the things you aren't sure if you should do."

CHAPTER Seventeen

The Amish Babysitter

It was a warm morning in June, and the sun was just coming up over the horizon. David drove up the long lane that led to the Miller's home. Sandra sat beside him in the front seat of their station wagon, with four sleepy children in the back seat. It was their first day of that summer, to be watched by their new babysitter, Esther. Sandra walked with them to the side door of the big farmhouse. Esther met them with wide open arms. "Good morning children. Come in and have a seat at the table. I've cooked bacon and eggs for your breakfast." Sandra handed her a box of cereal. "Esther, you shouldn't have gone to all the trouble. I brought cereal for them. We don't expect you to feed our four children breakfast and lunch all summer. I can bring oatmeal, poptarts, or cereal each day for their breakfasts." Esther was already setting plates and silverware on the table. "It's no trouble at all. They need a good hearty breakfast to grow big and strong." Sandra hugged the children and told them to behave. She turned to leave, but stopped at the door before walking out. "Thank you so much for everything, Esther. You are a Godsend and a blessing. We will pick the children up around four thirty."

The kitchen was very large and it had an old fashioned woodburning cookstove. The walls looked very plain without pictures or decorations on them. Ruthann noticed that the dish towel hanging on a knob and the one on Esther's arm, was plain white, unlike her mothers that had flowers and stripes on them. As she looked around the room, she noticed some other things that were different. The windows didn't have curtains. She spotted a big glass jar that had a metal handle on the side, and it looked like there was milk in it.

Esther asked them to bow their heads, and she gave thanks to the Lord for their food. Just after they opened their eyes, the kitchen door opened and Adam stepped in. He stopped just a couple feet inside the door and folded his arms. "Just who are these people sitting at my table, and who's sitting in my seat?" he asked, with a loud and gruff voice. All four children froze. Derek starred with his mouth wide open, Ruthann was wide eyed and quit chewing, and Miranda and Marjorie dropped their forks and were about to cry. "Now don't be tormenting the children so soon, Adam. You haven't even met them yet, and you've scared them stiff. Shame on you! Everything is okay children. This is my husband, Adam. He likes to pull pranks on people." Ruthann swallowed the food in her mouth and shook her head in disapproval, the twins grabbed each other's hand, and Derek burst out in laughter.

Adam walked over to the table where they were sitting. He smiled and patted Derek on the shoulder. Adam began to speak with a very soft and pleasant tone. "I guess I scared all of you, for a moment there. I hope that you are not angry with me. I'm so glad that you did not throw food at me too," Adam said, laughing. Derek knew that he liked him already. "Shucks, you didn't scare me a bit," he said, laughing back at him. "I'm okay, but I think it will take them a while to warm up to you," said Ruthann, pointing to her little sisters. The twins didn't want to talk to him, so they looked down at the table. "I'm not sitting in your seat, am I? Are you going to join us for breakfast?" asked Derek. "No to both questions, Derek. I was just pulling your leg, about sitting in my seat. I already ate this morning, before I did the chores." Derek was fascinated by this man that was able to pull one over on him, because he was always the one who pulled pranks on others, and did a very good job at it. "What kind of chores do you do, Mr. Miller?" he asked. "Children, you can call us by our first names. I'm Adam and she's Esther. I do many chores, but mainly, I feed and water the horses and cows, our dog, and the barn cats. The cats keep the mice population down." Ruthann got excited about the cats. "I love cats. Can I see them later?" she asked. Adam walked over to her. "Ruthann, most of the cats are wild and won't let people get near them, but we have a couple of tame ones. A week ago, one of them had kittens. I'll show them to you, and you can hold one." The twins looked up when he mentioned kittens. Adam walked over to them, and spoke in a gentle voice. "Marjorie and Miranda, would you like to hold a kitten too? There are two yellow ones and a white one." They both nodded their heads "yes" and gave bashful smiles. "Well, It was very nice to meet you, children. Now I must go to the buggy shop and get to work."

After breakfast, Esther told the children to follow her. She went outside and walked down the long sidewalk, and then stopped in front of a small stone building. "This building has a smoke house through that door on the left, and here in this room is where I make soap, in that stone trough." She explained how the soap was made and how they smoked their meat. They were so intrigued and full of questions. Esther loved children, and enjoyed teaching them new things. Their youngest daughter just got married, so they had an empty nest. Esther thought the home was too quiet now, so she welcomed the sounds of laughter and the pitter patter of the children's feet. She was so excited when she heard that Sandra needed a babysitter. Sandra's friend, Rachel, told her that Esther sold homemade butter and soap. Sandra met Esther when she went to her house to buy some butter. While she was there that day, she asked Esther if she knew of anyone who might be interested in watching her children.

On the way back to the house, she stopped at the well that had a hand pump. There was a windmill just a few feet behind it. "Wow! That is really cool! Can I climb the ladder up to the top of it?" asked Derek. "Nine! I mean no!" Esther quickly answered. "You must never climb the windmill. It is too dangerous, so you may not climb it. This is a rule for your own good. It is to protect you." Derek quietly asked Ruthann why Esther said "nine," at first. Esther heard him. "The word "nine" in our Dutch language means "no" in English. Come along, we must go back inside. It looks like it is going to rain hard." The grey clouds were rolling in fast. When they stepped into the house, it was so dark that they could hardly see. Esther lit a kerosene lantern so they could see better. That brought on questions from the children. Derek was fascinated at how she could turn the knob on the side to brighten and dim it. Ruthann didn't care for the smell. Miranda and Marjorie didn't understand why she didn't turn on a light somewhere. Esther didn't mind their curiosity at all, in fact she found it very amusing.

"Let's sit at the table, children. I Would like to get to know you better. I will ask you questions, and then you can ask me questions." Esther asked them how old they were, what their favorite foods were, and what things they like to do. "I like to work on cars with my dad," said Derek. "I like art and poetry," said Ruthann. "We like to play with dolls and play house," said Miranda. "And we like to help with real babies," added Marjorie. "Thank you for sharing those things with me. Now is there something you would like to ask me?" Ruthann asked why she used straight pins in her dress instead of buttons or zippers. Derek asked if they could have a buggy ride sometime, and the twins asked if she had any dolls to play with. "We use straight pins because we consider buttons and zippers as fancy things on clothing, and we believe we should dress very plain. We should be different from the rest of the world, and not conform to their ways. I'm sure we can take you on a buggy ride, if your parents give permission." Esther walked to a closet in the next room, and came back to the table with two dolls in her hand. She handed the Amish dressed girl and boy doll to the twins. They looked at them, and then looked at eachother with raised eyebrows. Esther saw the looks on their face and thought she better explain. "The dolls have plain faces because we dont believe in putting eyes, nose, mouth and other details on them. We think that it would be vain to try to make them look cute or pretty. If you are finished with questions, I'll show you some other rooms in the house." Ruthann just had to ask one more. "What is that glass thing over there with a handle? It looks like there's milk in it." Esther picked it up and sat it on the table in front of Ruthann. "I'm so glad you asked, because I think you can help me with it. You were right. There is milk in it, straight from the cow, so it has a lot of cream in it. When this handle is turned, it stirs the milk, and the cream in it will turn to butter. It is called a jar churn or butter churn. Go ahead and turn the handle." Ruthann turned it around and around until her hand was tired. The twins took a short turn each, and then Derek took his turn until the butter formed in it. "Look at that! I made it turn into butter because I'm the strongest," boasted Derek. "That is true that you are the strongest, Derek, but it is also true that all of you had a part in turning the cream to butter. It would have taken you longer, if the girls had not helped. I thank all of you for helping me. Follow me children."

Esther showed them the living room and bathroom. After that she led them into the great room, which was almost empty. She explained that the very large room was mainly used for church services and other large gatherings, like weddings. She explained that families in the Amish community that had large rooms like that, took turns having church services in their homes. The church benches were taken to the home in a large flatbed buggy, a day or two before each Sunday service.

The next room that they followed Esther into was the brightest room they had been shown. It had large windows all along the outside wall that looked out to the porch and the front yard. In the middle of the room was a long quilting stand with a nearly completed quilt on it. There was a long bench on each side so that several women could hand quilt it together. Ruthann thought that the quilt on it looked like a beautiful work of art. There were many different shades of green that swept across the fabric, like a grassy meadow that gradually turned into shades of teal and then aqua, like water that flowed into a deep blue sea. "It must have taken a long time to put all of those little white stitches all over the quilt! It's so pretty!" exclaimed Ruthann. "Yes, it does take quite a while. Next week there will be six ladies here, and we will spend time working on it together and finish it. The work they do that day to finish it, is no more important than the ladies who worked on it for only an hour or two in the past, because that was all the time they had to give. You see, it took every single stitch, from beginning to end, with many different people working on it, to get the job done. Every person played an important part in the completion of the quilt. Each little stitch was a small gift of love, for the young lady that we give it to, as a wedding gift. Never underestimate the small good deeds you do for others, because it can make a big difference in their lives."

The day seemed to go by so quickly for Esther. She had tears in her eyes as she and Adam watched the station wagon disappear down the lane. "Adam, it was a wonderful day! Thank you for agreeing that I should watch David and Sandra's children. They are such a blessing to have around, and it brings me much joy." Adam smiled and took her hand in his. "My dear Esther, I can clearly see that it does. I hope you feel the same way six months from now."

CHAPTER Eighteen

Mission Field Of Love

The next morning Sandra didn't have to prod the children to get up. Derek and Ruthann woke up on their own, and were dressed and sitting in the family room when she got up. The twins got up immediately, when she leaned in the doorway and called in to them to wake up.

The drive to the Miller's home was very different than it was the morning before. The children were bright eyed and bushy tailed. They were full of excitement about what new discoveries were in store for them on the Amish farm. "Quiet down a little back there!" yelled David. "We know you are excited, but your father and I want you all to calm down before we get there. It's still early, and I don't want you entering their home so rambunctious. You are to be on your best behavior today. Esther has been very kind to you, so you need to thank her with good behavior," ordered Sandra.

After breakfast Esther told the children that they could go out and play, but that they had to stay on the porch, or stay in the yard close to the house. They were given strict instructions not to go down the lane, in the fields, or in the barns.

Esther had some household chores to do, but she looked out the windows occasionally to check up on them. The twins were on the porch keeping busy, playing with the Amish dolls. Ruthann was walking around the flowerbeds and smelling the rose bushes. Derek was playing with their dog, Samson.

An hour had passed by, and Esther took a break from her shores to go outside and visit with the children. "Girls, have you given the dolls names yet? Oh my! What is this I see on the porch floor, coloring? You colored on the floor with your markers!" said Esther, shocked at what she saw. Marjorie excitedly spoke up. "Yes, we wanted to surprise you with pretty pictures of your cows, your horses, and cats, and dogs and-" Miranda interrupted her. "We put nice faces on the dolls too, not fancy ones, like you aren't supposed to." Esther put her hand over her mouth. She took a moment to process the situation, and then bent down and gently hugged the girls. "That Was very sweet of you. Now let's pick up the markers, and put them back in your bag. We need to find Ruthann and Derek. They were in sight, a little while ago."

Esther and the twins walked around the corner of the house, and almost bumped into Ruthann. She had an armful of roses and various other flowers. "Oh my, What have you done child?" Esther asked, with surprise. "I wanted to make you the biggest, and most beautiful bouquet you've ever seen," smiled Ruthann. Little did she know that Esther was waiting patiently since early spring for her favorite rose bush to bloom, so that her friends could see its beauty when they would visit that weekend. "How kind of you. Thank you so much." She didn't have the heart to explain to Ruthann, that the Amish prefer not to pick flowers for display in the home, but instead, to admire them outside as God intended them to be.

"Girls, did Derek tell you where he was going? I must find him." They didn't know where he went. Esther was beginning to worry that something bad may have happened to him. They walked all the way around the house, but he was nowhere to be found. She called his name and the girls joined in. They walked to the buggy barn, but Adam had not seen him. They walked to the horse barn, but he wasn't there either. As they got close to the well, Esther heard something. She asked the girls to be still. They all stood quietly for a moment, and then she heard the sound again. She was sure that it sounded like Derek giggling, but she looked around and didn't see him. "Look Esther! It's Derek. He's way at the top of the windmill," Miranda yelled, pointing up. "He's high up in the sky," laughed Marjorie. "I'm Tarzan!" shouted Derek, as he let go of the ladder, and beat on his chest. Esther instantly felt faint. "Derek!

Don't let go of the ladder like that again." she yelled, waving her arms frantically. "I'm not afraid! I can hide really well like him too. You guys walked right below me, and didn't know that I was here. I'm a good climber, and I'm pretending it's a tree," he bragged.

Esther couldn't believe what she saw, or what she was hearing. "Derek! Please! Hush and climb down very carefully and slowly." Derek began climbing down. "I'm okay, Esther. I'm not a baby like my scaredy cat sisters. I climbed up real fast." Esther held her breath and watched with both hands over her heart, until he was safely on the ground. "You will not feel okay, when you have to sit in a corner for the rest of the day," she said, with her hands on her hips. Derek never saw Esther with a frown on her face. He Knew he was in trouble. She grabbed him by his ear, and marched him into the house. The girls followed with wide eyes and mouths open. They were surprised to see her handling Derek that way. "You disobeyed my rule, not to climb the windmill. If you fell, it could have killed you. How do you think that would make everyone feel?" asked Esther. "Well I wouldn't feel anything, if I was dead," Derek said, with a snicker. "Do you think your parents would think it was funny, if when they got here, they had to pick up their son's dead body, put it in the car, and take it to the funeral home? They would be broken-hearted, that their only son was dead, and gone forever on this earth."

Derek became more serious and was taking in all that she was saying. Your sisters would have seen your twisted and bloody body, and would never be able to get that out of their minds. I would be ridden with guilt and shame the rest of my life, for not watching you more closely." Esther tried to think of everything she could, to make him understand how horrible the consequences could have been, from his disobedience. "Derek, you would never have the chance to play ball again with your friends, or work on cars with your father. You would never have the chance to grow up, get married, or have children. Your actions were selfish and disobedient. That does not please God." Esther was crying now as she spoke.

Derek had tears running down his cheeks. He wrapped his arms around Esther and sobbed. "I'm so sorry Esther. I shouldn't have climbed the windmill. I knew I shouldn't. Please! Don't cry anymore." Esther gently pulled his arms away from her sides, and wiped his face with her apron. "Come child, let's sit over here at the table." The girls were still standing at the entrance of the kitchen door, and they were taking it all in with tears in their eyes. Esther told Ruthann to place the flowers in the sink, and for them to sit down with her and Derek. "What shall we do now?" Esther asked, somberly. "You disobeyed, Derek, and I got very scared and angry. Shall I carry out the punishment that I mentioned earlier?" Both twins instantly said "Yes!" Ruthann put her hands over their mouths just as quickly. There was silence for a moment, and then Derek spoke. "Yes. You should make me sit in a corner for the rest of the day. I should also have to smell the roast beef and mashed potatoes that you fix for lunch, and do without. I deserve it. I'm sorry. I will never do that again, or break any other rule that you have." Esther was very soft hearted. She could tell that he was truly sorry, and had learned a lesson. "No. I don't believe that I will punish you. I forgive you, and I will give you an extra cookie for dessert instead." Derek looked at his sisters with confusion, and then back at Esther. "Did I hear you right? An extra cookie? Why would you do that, when I was so bad today?" Esther realized that she could use her decision as an example of Jesus' love for everyone. "Well, Derek, I just remembered what Jesus did for me. I disobeyed Him many times, but He forgave me and instead of hell, He gave me heaven. If we believe that Jesus died on the cross for our sins and ask Him to forgive us, and give our lives to live for Him, His blood will wash away every sin. Because He forgave me, then I should forgive you. You must learn that some bad things we do have consequences, even if we are forgiven. I will have to tell your parents what you did. That is a consequence that you will face this time. I will make sure that they know, you apologized and promised not to break rules anymore." With that, Derek gave a weak smile and thanked her.

David waited in the stationwagon with the girls while Esther, Derek, and Sandra discussed what happened that day. When they were walking out of the house and saying goodbye, they were all smiling. Ruthann was so glad to see that, because she didn't want to have another babysitter. She loved Esther the first day she met her.

When Adam came in from his busy day of building a new buggy, he found Esther laying on the living room couch. "Why are you sleeping at this hour of the day?" he asked, with concern. He helped her sit up, and sat down beside her. "Oh my! What a day I have had, my dear husband. You have no idea, I'm sure. The children were so well behaved and easy to care for yesterday, but today-" Adam interrupted. "I was afraid of that. I was concerned that they would be too much work for you. Children can take a lot of energy to care for, and we have already raised children that are adults now. Maybe you are too old for this job. You know that we don't need the money." Esther put her hand on his. "Adam, I assure you that I am not too old. We must remember that children can be far from perfect. They are learning so much as they grow up. We must try to be patient and teach them right from wrong." She was smiling and Adam knew that there was no way she was going to give up her job. "My sweet Esther, you are working on a mission field and your weapon is love." Adam kissed her on the cheek. "Adam, let's pray for them and their parents now. I don't want them to be too harsh with Derek for his behavior today. Sandra looked very tired when I talked with her. They both work so hard." Adam put his arm around her and they bowed their heads to pray.

The next morning Esther woke up earlier than usual. It was Friday morning, the end of the first week that Esther babysitted the Stewart children. Her daughter Sharon was visiting for the day, and wanted to meet them. She played tag, and walked around the farm with them. She showed them the horses and let them pet them. Derek especially liked the tour of the buggy barn. Adam was putting the wheels on a new buggy and let them climb inside of one. Sharon was very impressed at how polite and well behaved the children were. She was happy that her mother had them there to fill her days with joy.

After Sharon and Esther finished the dishes, Esther joined the children in the living room, and Sharon went to the bathroom. A few minutes later she joined them, and sat down next to Esther. They began having a serious conversation in Dutch. Ruthann had a feeling that they were talking about them. Esther stood up in front of the couch, where all four children were sitting. "Sharon has brought something to my attention. I have noticed the same thing, and it has happened too often this week. When she went to use the bathroom, the toilet was not flushed. You must do better with remembering to flush when you are finished. Who used the bathroom last?" There was no answer from the children. "Just be honest and admit that it was you, if you were the last one in there. Raise your hand if you went to the bathroom after lunch." They all raised their hands. Ruthann thought that it might have been her, because she went after Derek and she couldn't remember if she flushed or not. She wasn't going to admit to it though. She would be so embarrassed if Sharon thought that she had a habit of not flushing. "I almost always flush, even if I forgot this time," she thought to herself.

Sharon and Esther spoke in Dutch again. "You will all have to sit here until someone admits to it," said Esther. Derek stood up and looked at his sisters. "I remember flushing after I went. Come on you guys, admit to it so we can go out and play!" The twins said they saw each other flush. "Was it you that didn't flush Ruthann?" asked Esther. "No!" she answered. Ruthann decided that she wasn't going to admit to it, even if they had to sit there for a year! She felt sorry for her innocent siblings, but most of all for not being honest with Esther, who was so kind to her. They sat for four hours until their parents picked them up.

CHAPTER Nineteen

A Buggy Ride To Church

David and Sandra had plans to go away for a weekend to celebrate their anniversary. Esther offered to babysit so they could go alone. The Stewart children had the opportunity to attend an Amish church service with Esther and Adam on Sunday morning. They rode in Adam's large buggy to the church service, which was held at an Amish home that was five miles away. It was definitely an interesting, and exciting experience for them.

Derek and Sandra had a wonderful time together that weekend also. Their family was back home together that Sunday evening before bedtime. They all gathered in the living room and talked about their weekend. "How was the buggy ride to the church?" asked David. "The horses went clip clop, clip clop," said Marjorie. "It was really bumpy too," said Miranda. "It was a lot of fun!" added Ruthann. "Adam let me hold the reins for a while," David said, with excitement.

"Derek, what was the church service like?" Sandra asked, with interest. "It was like our church in that there wasn't any music when they sang. They sing in Dutch but we knew what songs they were singing, because they were the same tune as our hymns at church." Sandra thought that was very interesting. "Ruthann, what did you find interesting or different about it?" She thought for a moment. "Well the families didn't sit together. The women sat on one side of the room, and the men on the other. The benches didn't have backs on them, so you

could see people do stuff that you can't see them do at our church. Oh, and of course they all wore plain clothing, without print on them. A girl about my age kept turning around and staring at me. I think she was counting every flower on my dress," she said, laughing.

David asked the twins what they thought. "I saw lots of cute babies and we got to hold one," said Miranda. "Everyone ate lunch together when church was over," said Marjorie. "Well, your mother and I had a wonderful weekend also. We did some hiking at the state park, and went canoeing in the river. We want to take you children there next time. Now, before we say goodnight, let's all bow our heads and I'll lead in prayer. Heavenly father, thank you for the opportunity to have an unforgettable,wonderful weekend with my wife. Thank you Father for protecting our children over the weekend, and thank you for Esther and Adam, and what a blessing they are to our family. We love you. May we all get a good night's sleep. In Jesus name we pray. Amen."

CHAPTER Twenty

Bible School Days

erek and Ruthann learned Bible stories from Sunday school classes and summer Bible school. The Bible school was in the morning from eight a.m. until noon each day, for a week in the summer. One day at Bible school, when Ruthann was ten, she had a terrifying experience. She had just got over a very bad cold, but she had a bit of a cough still lingering. She assured her mother that morning that she felt well enough to go to Bible school that day anyway.

It was recess time, when the children would get a chance to use the restroom, stretch their legs, and play outside. After jumping rope for a few minutes in the church parking lot, Ruthann went to the restroom with her girlfriend, Carla. The girls were washing their hands, when Ruthann began coughing. Her coughing was so intense that Carla wasn't sure she'd ever stop, and then all of a sudden she did stop. Carla was relieved for a moment, but then Ruthann began gasping for air. "Ruthie what's wrong?" yelled Carla. Ruthann shook her head "no," and pointed at her throat. Carla grabbed her arm, and ran up the basement stairs with her. "We have to hurry and get to Ezra. Run faster Ruthie," cried Carla, in desperation. When they got outside, to the back of the church, they saw Ezra standing by a tree. He was watching the boys play softball. Ruthann knew she couldn't hold on much longer, and was so afraid that she was choking to death. Ezra didn't see the girls running towards him, so it startled him when Ruthann grabbed his arm and tugged at him frantically. At first he looked at her in surprise, and then the fear in his eyes scared her even more. Ruthann was turning blue and holding her throat. "She can't breathe, Ezra!" yelled Carla. The next thing Ruthann knew, she was upside down being shook like a salt shaker by Ezra. He shook her with one arm, and he was hitting her on the back with his other. She coughed up a big glob of phlegm that had been lodged in her throat. She came to the realization that she was alright, and that the boys could probably see her underpants because her dress was over her head. She wanted him to let her go, so she yelled at Ezra. "Let me down! I'm okay now," Ruthann cried, as she tried to cover herself. He wouldn't stop so she started tugging on his pant leg, while trying to push her dress up over her bottom. He didn't want this child in his care to die, and was so frantic that he didn't hear her! By that time the boys had stopped playing ball, and Derek ran up to Carla. He saw that his sister was wanting down, so he walked up to Ezra. "You can put Ruthie down now. She said that she's okay." Ezra stopped hitting her back, and apologized while turning her upright. Ruthann ran away, not giving him a chance to talk to her. She was very thankful for what Ezra did for her, but all she wanted to do is run away and hide. The humiliation of the boys seeing her upside down with her dress over her head, was more than she could bear at the time. Carla ran after her and followed her into the restroom where the whole thing began. "Ruthie are you okay?" she asked, with sniffles from crying. "I thought you were going to die, so I was praying for you the whole time. Please come out of the stall and talk to me." Ruthann blew her nose and wiped her eyes, before stepping out. Her face was blotchy and her eyes were red from crying. "I am so embarrassed Carla! The boys will be talking about me and laughing." Carla put her arm around her friend. "I think you are wrong about that Ruthie. Remember our Bible memory verse for today? Be ye kind one to another. I'm sure they will remember that. The boys might talk about how Ezra saved your life though. Besides, you know that if Derek heard any mean talk about you, that he'd take care of them for sure!"

It was Friday, the last day of Bible School. Sandra gave the children permission to ride their bikes there and back home. Derek and Ruthann invited their neighbor friends, Josh and Jamie, to go with them as their visitor's, and they rode their bikes to Bible school with them. When it was time to go home, Ezra offered them all a ride home in his van, because the clouds were dark and it looked like it was going to rain. They were all excited about riding their bikes home together, so they assured him that they would go straight home, and that they didn't mind if they got a little wet. They got a quarter of a mile down the road, when Derek and Josh suddenly stopped. The girls almost ran into them. Derek turned his bike around to face them. "I left my new baseball mitt outside on the old stump, behind the church at recess. I have to go back and get it. Josh, you go ahead with the girls, and I'll catch up with you." Josh turned his bike around. "No way! I'm not riding alone with a bunch of girls. I'm going with you." Ruthann got off her bike, and grabbed the back of Derek's shirt. "You promised mom and dad that you wouldn't leave us girls alone. They even told you not to ride way ahead of us. We are all supposed to stay together! " Derek looked at Josh and then back at the girls. "Okay everybody, we're going back to the church together. Ruthie hurry up and get back on your bike. Lets go!" Off they went. By the time they arrived at the church, everyone had left. Derek got his glove, and when they all headed out of the church parking lot it began to sprinkle. The wind was blowing harder and there was lightning in the distance. Marjorie was lagging behind, and Miranda screamed every time she heard the thunder. Ruthann looked back at the twins. "Miranda, quit screaming!" she said, screaming at both sisters, "Can't you ride a little faster Marjorie?" Derek looked back at the girls, and couldn't believe his eyes. There in the distant field behind them, was a funnel cloud. He didn't want to scare the girls, but he knew that they had to hurry and get to shelter. "You have to ride faster girls!" he yelled, at the top of his lungs. Miranda started crying. "We can't! It's too windy," yelled marjorie. Derek told Josh that there was a tornado behind them but not to say anything, and to stay in the lead. Josh looked back and with wide eyes, kept peddling. "I'm going to ride close to the twins, and try to calm them down," said Derek. Ruthann saw the dark swirling cloud in the distance, when she turned to look at the twins again. She knew that Derek saw it too by the look on his face, when he passed by her to ride with the twins. She told Jamie who was riding beside her, and gave her the signal to keep quiet. They rode a little further but the wind was blowing harder by the minute which made it almost impossible to peddle. It began to hail, and all of the girls were screaming. Derek got off his bike, and yelled for them all to do the same. The twins could barely stay standing from the force of the wind, and they had their hands over their faces for protection from the sting of the hail. Derek grabbed their arms, and ran to the ditch. They tumbled in because it was so steep. Josh and the other girls followed, leaving their bikes on the road. Derek yelled something to them, but they couldn't hear him from the roaring sound around them. They all lay face down as dust, branches, and other debris blew over them. "Just stay down!" Derek yelled, as loud as he could. Ruthann grabbed Jamie's hand, and began praying out loud. "Dear God please keep us safe. I know that you have the power to stop this storm and the tornado. I know you love us, and always hear our prayers. In today's Bible story you commanded the winds to be still, and they obeyed. I believe in your power, and that you are here with us now. Please protect us all. In Jesus name I pray. Amen." Suddenly there was calm and quietness. When they climbed out of the ditch, they looked at the sky and saw a beautiful full rainbow, and the sun began to peek out of the clouds. They all began to cheer and gave each other hugs. The twins jumped up and down and clapped their hands. "It's a pretty rainbow!" yelled Marjorie. "It's a promise from God!" yelled Miranda. "That tornado behind us looked so cool!" said Josh. "It sure was! I can't wait to tell dad," said Derek. He started laughing so hard that he doubled over, holding his stomach. "What's got into you, man?" Josh asked, feeling left out of a joke. "You all look like muddy clowns. You have mud all over your faces and clothes!" They all looked at eachother and joined him in laughter.

Their bikes were scattered on the road, but when they got on them, they were all rideable. They were only a short distance from Jami and Josh's house, so it didn't take them long to get there. When they arrived, Jamie thanked Ruthann for praying. "I didn't realize how powerful God is. At first I thought we were all going to die, but He protected us. Thank you for inviting us to Bible School too. It was fun, and I learned some stuff from the Bible. I still don't understand why you always wear dresses though. You and the twins' dresses were blowing up to your waist back there!" They both laughed. "It's not the first time that's happened to me, and I doubt it will be the last," Ruthann hollered back at her, while riding off towards home.

The children didn't have a babysitter that week. They were in Bible school most of the day, and promised to behave until their parents got home from work. By the time Sandra and David got home, the children had taken showers, and were sitting on the porch. As they pulled into the lane, Sandra mentioned to David, how sweet the children looked. David told her how proud he was of them to be able to leave them alone for a while, and to trust them to ride their bikes straight home after Bible school. "I bet they rode into some rain though. Look how wet everything is," David pointed out. When they got out of the car, the children ran to them, and talked excitedly at the same time. David let Derek talk first. He just about covered everything that happened on their bike ride home from Bible school. Ruthann told them that he left one thing out. She told them about her prayer. David motioned for the family to gather around him, and they had a family hug. When the twins tried to squirm away, he asked them to stay a little longer. Everyone closed their eyes while he said a prayer of thanks to the Lord for keeping them safe.

CHAPTER Twenty - One

Oh Happy Day

The summer before Ruthann started fifth grade, she understood God's plan of salvation. She wanted to give her life to Jesus. She knew that she was a sinner, and that she needed to ask forgiveness for her sins. She felt the guilt and heavy weight of her sins, yet she put off confessing them for several weeks. Finally one day, when she was in the house alone, she knelt by her parent's bedside. She wanted to be free of her sins, and to know that if she died that she would go to Heaven and not hell. Ruthann began to pray a simple, yet life changing prayer. "God, I'm sorry for my sins. Please forgive me. I believe that your Son Jesus, died on the cross for everyone. I want to give my life to you, and obey your commandments. Thank you Jesus, for dying on the cross to wash away my sins. I love you. Amen."

Ruthann stood up, and wiped the tears from her eyes. There was an abundant joy in her heart, like she never knew before. A heavy weight was lifted from her shoulders, and she felt a peace that made her feel so loved and secure. She believed completely, that if she accepted the gift of salvation through the blood of Jesus, that her past, present, and future sins would be forgiven, and that she would live for eternity in Heaven.

The first thing Ruthann wanted to do was run to the tree swing in the backyard. She went there often when she wanted to be alone, and think about things. She began to swing so high, that she felt like she could fly right into the arms of Jesus. She began singing. "Thank you Lord for saving my soul. Thank you Lord for making me whole. Thank you Lord for giving to me, thy great salvation so rich and free." She was so thankful and full of joy that she felt like she would burst, if she didn't sing out praises to the Lord. She sang many hymns on the swing that day. The songs she sang at church in the past, became real and personal to her. It was like she truly understood them, for the first time. She really meant what she was singing.

At the supper table that evening, Ruthann told her family about accepting Jesus as her Savior. With tears in their eyes, Sandra and David got up from the table and hugged her. "Oh praise God! Your father and I have been praying that you would ask Jesus into your heart and live for Him." David took Sandra's hand and kissed her. "My dear wife, that is two of our children born again now, and two more to go." David gently tapped the twins heads. Marjorie and Miranda were so excited. They knew that it was something that the big girls and boys did, and they had many questions for their older sister. "How did you feel after you told Jesus you were sorry for sinning so much?" asked Miranda. "Did you try to remember and tell him about all of them Ruthie?" asked Marjorie. Derek rushed into the conversation before she could answer the twins. "Ding dong. God always sees everything, so she didn't need to list her sins. He even knows what people are thinking too." The twins ignored their older brother's comment and kept asking questions. "You get to wear the head cover like mom wears, don't you?" asked Miranda. "You have to wear your hair up in a bun now too," added Marjorie. Derek got saved a year before Ruthann, so he thought of more details to add to the list of new things that she was required to do after being saved. "Don't forget that you will need to get baptized soon. Oh, and you will be taking communion once a month at church, and you will have to wash an old lady's stinky feet. The first time I washed feet, it was so gross! Two men had their feet washed in the same water, and there was fuzz, hair, and scummy toe jam in it," said Derek, wrinkling his nose. Just the thought of that made Ruthann feel nauseous. David turned his back on them, and was trying very hard not to laugh out loud. Sandra began scolding Derek. "Now, young man, you stop that kind of talk right now! It's an act of obedience and a sign of love and humility, to wash a brother and sister in Christ's feet. Jesus did it with the disciples at the Last Supper."

CHAPTER Twenty - Two

Questions

Although the Mennonite ways had become the normal way of life for the Stewart family, there were questions and doubts that Ruthann was having, as she began her fifth grade year at school. She had accepted Jesus as her Savior that summer, and was baptized by the preacher with sprinkling of water over her head. It was a sign of obedience to the Lord and was a testimony that she was saved by grace, through the shedding of His Blood on the cross, for her sins. It was after that, when she would be expected to wear a covering on her head. She was so happy that Jesus now lived in her heart. She knew that the Holy Spirit was in her and would guide her, but she still had doubts and dread about the head covering. Being different with how she dressed, how she wore her hair, and with things she wasn't allowed to do, caused her to stand out, and be singled out. Now that she had to wear the head covering, it would draw even more attention to her being different. She wanted to wear her long, wavy hair down, instead of in braids, which took some persuasion. Sandra told her that if it really meant that much to her, then she could wear her hair the way she wanted to. Most of the Mennonite women wore their hair up in a bun, with the covering over it. She made up her mind that if she wore the covering to school, that she certainly was not going to wear her hair in a bun!

A question she always wanted to ask Ezra was "Why do the girls have to look so different, and the boys look and dress like everyone else?" It didn't seem fair to her that things were so hard on the girls, and that the boys had it so easy. They weren't made fun of, and didn't have to feel different than the other boys.

Ruthann also wondered why her church didn't allow a piano or any other musical instruments. When she visited a Baptist church years ago, they had a piano and an organ. Didn't she read in the Bible, that instruments were played for the Lord? She also wondered why it was thought to be a sin for men to have long hair. Every picture she ever saw of Jesus showed Him with long hair. Then there was the issue of drinking. Of course she knew it was wrong to be drunk with wine, but was it a sin to drink a glass of wine? She read in the Bible that Jesus turned the water into wine. There were so many rules that she had to follow because she was a Mennonite. Rules that she didn't find in the Bible.

The day had come that Ruthann was dreading so much. She loved school, but she had a lot of anxiety about going that morning. It was Ruthann's first day in fifth grade. It took her a week to decide on which dress to wear, and she finally made up her mind, not to wear the covering on her head until the next day.

"Ruthann why aren't you eating your breakfast?" asked Deana, the new babysitter. Before she could answer Derek chimed in. "She can't wait to see her boyfriend." He fluttered his eyelashes and laughed. Ruthann stood up with her hands on her hips. "I don't have a boyfriend!" she said, angrily. Deana shook her finger at Derek and scolded him. "You know it's not nice to aggravate your sister. Now stop teasing her." Miranda raised her hand. "Yes. What would you like to say, Miranda? There's no need to raise your hand. You are not in school, you know," said Deana, impatiently. "Yes ma'am, but you sound like a mean teacher, and I don't want to get in trouble. I just want to say, why I think Ruthie isn't eating her breakfast. I think it's because she's scared." Marjarie raised her hand, and then with a scared look on her face, she quickly put her hand down. Derek couldn't stop giggling at his sisters, and Ruthann was scowling because everyone was talking like she wasn't there. "Marjorie, what is it?" With tears forming in her eyes, Marjorie quietly answered. "I'm scared too. It's our first day in second grade," she cried. Deana marched over to Marjorie. "Are you going to cry like a little baby? Second graders don't cry! You wipe your eyes, and finish your oatmeal this instant. All of you children eat, and I don't want to hear another word out of you. Do you understand?" Ruthann was still standing with her hands on her hips, and was furious. "What I understand is that my sister Miranda is right. You are mean!" With that, Ruthann sat down. "Mean or not, you children will obey me," said Deana, as she pushed Ruthann's chair further in. Derek spooned his oatmeal into his cup, and put a paper napkin over it while Deana was scolding Marjorie. The twins were both wiping their eyes, and never did eat their breakfast. Ruthann ate every bite and told Deana that she liked oatmeal, even though she didn't. She didn't want to give Deana the satisfaction of making her eat it.

Deana told the children to go outside to watch for the school bus. She was looking forward to ending her first morning with the Stewart children. It was sprinkling outside, so she decided she would watch them from the front window as they waited on the bus. Before she even made it to the window to look out, she heard the girls yelling. She couldn't believe what she saw! There on the hood of her car, stood Gabby their goat. The girls were yelling at it to get off, and were trying to swat it with their books, while Derek was bent over with laughter. Deana grabbed the broom from the kitchen closet and ran outside. When she got to her car, she yelled at the goat, and began swinging the broom at it. The goat jumped around on the hood of her car as though it was playing with her. Now all of the children were laughing, as she tried her best to remove Gabby from her car.

"Here comes the bus!" hollered Derek. When the bus stopped and the door opened, Gabby jumped down from the car, ran past the children, and jumped onto the steps of the bus. The bus driver grabbed the goat by the collar and held it there, until Derek took it from him and led the goat to the barnyard. He ran back to the bus as fast as he could. Every child on the bus was out of their seats and were cheering for Derek. When he saw their reaction, he felt like a hero. He raised his arms in the air, showed his muscles, and then gave a bow. The twins got on the bus while Derek was putting Gabby in the barnyard, but Ruthann was being lectured by Deana about how unruly she thought they all were, and that her parents were going to have to pay for the damage to her car. Ruthann finally just walked away from her while she was still talking. She knew that the bus driver would be leaving very soon, and she didn't want to be left behind with their new unhappy babysitter all day long. She was so embarrassed as she walked down the aisle, and made sure not to look anyone in the face. She was so relieved when she found an empty seat by a window. "That stupid goat!" She thought. That's just what she didn't want, more attention. These days she just wanted to be unnoticed, unlike when she was younger and wanted to be noticed all the time. She got up the courage to look around in the bus, to make sure that the twins were okay. She spotted them two rows back on the other side. They were smiling, and chatting away with each other. She was relieved that they weren't upset, but she suddenly felt so all alone. She didn't have any friends on the bus, and it was rare that anyone talked to her at all, until she got to school.

The day seemed to be going much better, until the long recess after lunch. Ruthann and Carla were walking through the playground when the fourth grade teacher, Mr. Clark, walked up to them. Mr. Clark was liked by all children in every grade, and they were always glad when he was with them outside at recess. He loved children, and it was a joy for him to play and talk with them. His wife couldn't have children, so to him the kids at school were like his children.

"Hi Ruthie. Hi Carla. How are you girls today?" His smile was the best feature about the short and pudgy, middle-aged man. There was never a doubt that his smile, or his questions were genuine. He made Ruthann feel accepted in spite of her differences, and she felt special when he spoke to her so kindly. "We're fine." Both girls said, at the same time and giggled. "Oh, that's very good to hear, but there's something different about one of you today. He looked at Carla with a smile, and patted her on the shoulder. "Your new little white cap looks very cute on you. And may I ask why you are wearing it today?" Carla looked a little embarrassed at first, and then she smiled. "Sure. Well, in our church, after a girl gets saved and baptised, she is supposed to wear it. We call it a covering. Ruthie got saved and was baptized on Sunday too." He looked at Ruthann and then back at Carla. "What a brave soul you are, Carla! I am so proud of you. You did what was right by being obedient, and doing what you were supposed to, even if it was hard to do." Ruthann was horrified! What must he think of her, for not wearing her covering? Mr. Clark turned to Ruthann. "Dear, why didn't you wear yours?" She was staring at the ground, crushed and fighting back the tears. Even if she knew what to say to him, she could barely speak. She finally looked up at him. "Because, because I -" She ran away as fast as she could so they wouldn't see her cry. The girls restroom was always a good place to go to when she wanted to disappear.

Ruthann felt so glad to be home, when she got off the bus that day. She ran to her bed, and had another good cry. She shared a bedroom with the twins, so she didn't have much privacy. They saw that she was crying and ran to tell their mother. Sandra entered the bedroom and sat on the bed next to Ruthann. "What's the matter sweetie? Was Derek teasing and tormenting you again today? I've been meaning to talk to him. He goes a little too far with it I know, but just keep in mind that he doesn't have a brother to play with, and he just wants attention." Wiping her eyes, Ruthann rolled over and sat up. "Oh, momma, I wish Esther didn't get sick, and that she was still our babysitter! We miss her so much. Deana is horrible, and the whole day was just horrible! She buried her head on her mother's shoulder. "I will have a talk with your father about Deana. Derek and your sisters aren't very happy about her either."

After telling her mother about the terrible things that happened that day, Ruthann felt much better. "I'm sorry that I laughed, when you told me your interpretation of what happened with Gabby this morning. When Deana told her side of the story, she just focused on the damage to her car. I understand how you were embarrassed by it but trust me, someday when you are older, you will look back at this and laugh about it too. As far as wearing your covering goes, well, I think that is a decision you have to make. I won't make you wear it. It's up to you." Ruthann gave her mother a hug. "Thank you, momma. I will wear it tomorrow. Carla won't feel so alone being different. I don't want to wear my hair in a bun like her though. I don't like how buns look on me, and you know how I got headaches, when I wore it up a few times." Sandra stroked her long, wavey, brown hair. "Yes. I do dear. I want to warn you that some of the children at school won't understand why you are wearing the covering, and some may poke fun at you. Just ignore it and go on. You will find out who your true friends are. I even had adults at my work, make fun of me for wearing my covering and long dresses. I just ignored them." Ruthann leaned her head on her mother's arm. "I love you mom," she said. "I love you too Ruthann," said Sandra.

CHAPTER Twenty-Three

The Bully

"Can Derek, the twins, and I ride our bikes to Westfield? The twins did real good the last time we all went. We have been saving the money that grandma Ethel gave us. We want to buy some bags of penny candy at the gas station. Mr. Johnson is very nice to us." Ruthann waited for the answer, while Sandra reached into her purse. "Yes. You can, but I want you children to be back in an hour. Here's a dollar. Get four packs of juicy fruit gum for me, please. Be careful and watch over your sisters." In a flash, Ruthann ran to tell her sisters and brother that they could ride their bikes to Westfield. All the way there, the girls followed Derek, and rode single file on the edge of the road. When they arrived, Derek told the twins to choose their candy first. They each had fifty cents. Mr. Johnson stood patiently behind the glass counter. It was filled with an assortment of penny candy, candy bars, and gum. The twins took five minutes each to decide on their choice of candy, and when they were done, they had a full lunch-size paper bag of candy. Ruthann took almost as long, but Derek was quick. He always got the same thing each time. The mechanic was on his break, and watched in amazement at how patient and kind Mr. Johnson was with the four Stewart children. After they left, he told Mr. Johnson that the kids would really get on his nerves taking so long to pick out their candy, and bagging it up for them piece by piece. "Awe, I really enjoy it. It sure makes my day to see their little faces light up. They get so excited with each choice. It brings so much pleasure to their simple little lives.

Mr. Johnson lost his wife and two young children in a car accident. He developed a drinking problem, and almost lost his business because of it. When the Stewart children found out that he lost his family, they wanted to reach out to him and give him gifts. The last time they were there Ruthann gave him a plan of salvation tract, and the twins gave him coloring pages that they colored. Derek gave him a Hot Wheels truck that looked just like his truck, that was parked at the station every day but Sunday. One day, he thought that he couldn't go on another single day. He was tired of life, and of the pain he felt in his heart, from the loss of his family. Sitting in the truck with his gun in his hand, he was about to end his life. The wind came in through the open window and it blew a paper from the dash onto his lap. He stared at it for a moment. It was the tract that Ruthann had given to him. He never read it before, but now he was curious why the little girl wanted him to have it. He put the gun down and picked up the tract, and began reading it. He couldn't stop. The message in it spoke of faith, hope, forgiveness, new life, and joy. It told him that God loved him enough to send His own son Jesus to save him. It told of God's promises. God knew how he felt with the loneliness and pain. He would always be beside him, and hear his prayers. He was not alone! Right then and there, with tears running down his face, he asked Jesus into his heart. Ever since that night, he was a new man, born again. He had a peace that he never had before, and a love for others. He began sharing with others what Jesus did for him, and was determined to lead the mechanic to Jesus someday too.

Early the next morning Ruthann woke up, when her father turned on the bedroom light. He walked around the room singing an old song that he heard his father sing years ago. "Froggy went a courtin, he did ride. Gun and pistol by his side -" She was definitely a morning person like her father. She jumped out of bed and began singing with him. The twins shared the same bedroom with her, and they were not so happy to wake up that way. Derek ran into the room and jumped at the foot of the twins' bed to help wake them up. When they wouldn't get up, he pulled the covers off them. Marjorie and Miranda began screaming. "Daddy, make him stop!" cried Miranda. "We're still sleepy," cried Marjorie. David grinned, and motioned for their laughing brother to leave the room.

As Ruthann brushed her hair, she wondered what the day at school would have in store for her. She put the tightly netted, white covering on the back of her head. It came up just high enough on top of her head to be seen from the front also. She picked up one straight pin and poked it through the edge of the cap. She weaved it in and out, grabbing just enough hair to hold it into place. She did the same thing on the other side, and tugged on it to make sure it was secure. She thought about how horrible it would be, if the wind blew it off her head while outside at recess. She stared at herself in the mirror, and thought that the covering made her look older. She wondered if she had to act more serious now. She wondered if the other boys and girls would ignore her, make fun of her, or keep asking her why she was wearing the covering. "I'm doing this for you, God. Please, be with me and help me through the day," she prayed, silently. She took a deep breath and walked into the kitchen. When she sat at the table, the others stopped eating and stared at her. "What's the matter with you guys? What are you staring at? You act as though you've never seen anyone wearing a covering before. I guess, I might as well get used to the staring. I just didn't expect to get it from my brother and sisters!" Talking with his mouth full of toast, Derek patted her on the shoulder. "Wow, Ruthie, you look pretty good with a fish net on your head." Miranda got up to touch it. Marjorie did the same. "I think you look pretty with it on," said Marjorie. Miranda Agreed.

The children got on the bus. Ruthann tried not to look at anyone in the eye. She sat in a seat halfway back, with a younger girl that lived down the road. Only a few empty seats remained when they got on the bus, so there wasn't an empty seat for three, to sit with the twins. Derek's friend Josh always saved him a seat in the back.

Two girls, sitting three rows ahead of her, kept turning around and laughing. Ruthann knew that they were laughing at her. She looked down and tried to ignore them. She wished she could snap her finger, and instantly be at school in her classroom. Two older boys that were sitting in front of her, joined in on the laughing when they caught on to what the girls were laughing at. One of the boys turned around, and asked her why she was wearing the beanie on her head. Ruthann looked down at her lap and ignored him. "Hey girlie, I asked you a question, and you better answer me," he said, slamming his hand on the back of the seat. Ruthann looked up at him. "Turn around and mind your own business!" She said, and looked back down hoping that he would give up. The next thing she knew, there was a tug on her head. When she looked up, he had her covering in his hand. He was laughing and waving it in the air above his head. She was so humiliated and scared, that she didn't even try to get the covering back from him. She was angry at him, and even more angry at herself, for not being able to hold back the tears. She began sobbing with her hands over her face, and bent her head down on the seat in front of her to hide it. She wanted to simply disappear.

Next to a window and across the aisle from Ruthann, sat a high school girl. She was trying to catch up on some unfinished homework, so she didn't see the whole thing happen. She looked up from her reading, when she heard someone sobbing. She saw Ruthann bent over, and hiding her face while crying. She figured out what was going on when she saw the boy wearing the covering on his head, and the other boy was laughing with him. She got out of her seat, and told him to give it back to Ruthann. "Who do you think you are? You're not my boss!" he said, laughing, and then took it off his head and sat on it. The high school girl asked Ruthann to scoot over, and sat in the seat beside her. She grabbed the boy from behind and did a head lock on him with one arm, and pulled his ear with her other hand as hard as she could. "You ought to know better than to pick on girls, Bradley! You big bully! I'll let you go, when you say you'll give it back to her." He squirmed and tried to get away. She just pulled harder. "Okay, okay! Let go! I'll give it back!" She let go of him, and gave him a slap on the back of the head. He turned around, and threw the covering back at her. She put her arm around Ruthann, and gave her a kleenex from her pocket. "Are you okay?" she asked. Ruthann nodded "yes" and wiped her eyes. "He's a big bully, and would be afraid to pick on anyone his own size. My boyfriend and I will make sure that he never bothers you again. Here's your cap, but I'm afraid that it's a little wrinkled. Can I help you put it on or something?" she asked, as she handed the covering to Ruthann. She took the covering, and bent it back into shape. "No. I'll put it back on when I get to school. Thank you for helping me. I'll be alright now that I know he won't bother me again," Ruthann said, as she wiped her tears. Just then Derek walked up to her seat. "Hi Brenda. Hey, Ruthie, what's going on? I heard someone say that you were crying." Brenda stood up, and sat back in her seat across the aisle, so he could sit down by Ruthann. Brenda explained everything to Derek. "Thanks for helping my sister, Brenda. Where'd Bradley go? I should punch his lights out!" Derek looked around and spotted him in the front seat. "The big sissy ran up front. Well, Ruthie, now you have three of us, who will make sure that he never bothers you again."

When the bus got to the school, Ruthann ran straight to the restroom. One of the straight pins was lost when the covering was pulled off her head. She made do with just one, and pinned it in the middle, at the top. She met Carla at the bottom of the big staircase, which led up to the third through fifth grade classrooms. Carla took Ruthann's hand. "Ruthie while you were in the restroom, I heard some kids from your bus talking about what happened to you on the way here. That was so mean of that boy! I heard that his name is Bradley, and he's in sixth grade. I'm proud of you for wearing your covering to school. Others will wonder about it and stare, but they will get used to it and so will we. We can talk more at recess okay?" Ruthann managed a smile. "Okay Carla. Thank you. You are a good friend!"

That day at school seemed to last forever. Most of her classmates didn't say anything about the covering on her head. They just stared, and avoided talking to her at all. Ruthann sat in the front seat of the bus going home. She was so glad that she didn't have to look at Bradley the whole way home. It was obvious to Sandra that something was wrong with Ruthann that evening. She was unusually quiet, and didn't eat much supper. "Derek, Marjorie, and Miranda, I want you to go outside and do your chores. Girls, make sure that you get all of the eggs this time. Ruthann, I want you to stay inside, and help me with the dishes."

Ruthann was still very quiet as she dried the dishes. "Would you like to talk about what's on your mind, Ruthann? I can tell that something has upset you," said Sandra, as she washed the last dish. Ruthann couldn't hold back the tears, but she kept drying the plate in her hand. She cleared her throat, and finally stopped and looked at her mother. "Why does it have to be so hard?" she asked, slamming the dish towel down. "What do you mean exactly?" asked Sandra. "Being a Mennonite and being a Christian. We always stand out like a sore thumb. A lot of people shy away from us. We have to put up with rude comments and unkind behavior, and turn the other cheek. Just once, I'd like the satisfaction of punching one of them in the face!" said Ruthann, with clenched fists. With that comment being said, Sandra could see her daughter's father in her, a little fighter. "Why, Ruthann! Do you think that would do any good at all? You wouldn't be any better than the person who was being unkind to you, and it surely wouldn't be what Jesus would do. It's okay to get angry, but how you handle that anger is very important. Even Jesus got angry at the people buying and selling in the Temple, God's House. He didn't hit or hurt people. What has happened today?" Sandra asked, as she put her arm around her angry daughter. Ruthann didn't want to worry her mother with the issue, but now that she asked, she would tell her. She told her every detail about what happened on the bus, and asked her if she had to keep wearing the covering. "My sweet Ruthann, I'm so sorry that you had to go through that on the bus this morning. First of all, I don't want you to ever hesitate to tell me anything, just because you think it will worry or upset me. I am your mother and I am here for you to talk to, always. I love you very much! As far as wearing your covering or not, I am leaving that up to you. You need to pray and think about it, and make the decision yourself. You have another choice to make. You can let the bullying, people poking fun, and leaving you out, break you or make you stronger. It's hard to stand alone on what you believe is right, but it is very important to stay true to that belief, and not give in to peer pressure." Ruthann wrapped her arms around Sandra. "I love that about you so much, mom! You don't force me to wear my hair up or to wear a covering like some of the other moms at church do. You let me do what I want to as long as it doesn't hurt anyone, and you don't scold or judge me harshly, if I want to do things differently. Thank you for loving me just the way I am, and giving me the freedom to just be me! I love you mom!" Sandra called the other children inside. After their baths, she read to them on her bed, from their favorite book. Before telling the children goodnight, she talked with them for a while. "Mom, where is dad this evening? Is he working late again?" asked Derek. "Yes, Derek.

Your father is working late every night this week." Ruthann thought that her mother looked sad. "I don't like it when daddy works late!" cried Marjorie. "I don't either," agreed Miranda. "Are you okay mom?" asked Ruthann, concerned. "I'm fine, dear. I'm just very tired." Sandra yawned. In a few seconds her eyes closed, and she fell fast asleep. "Come on you guys. Lets go to bed. Ruthie make sure that you gently close the door when we walk out," ordered Derek. The Twins silently followed him out of the room with Ruthann right behind them.

CHAPTER Twenty - Four

Saved From The Fire

andra and David Found that life in the old country house was more difficult in the winter. It was hard to keep a couple of the rooms in the house warm enough, so they closed a section off. David got up on a cold January morning to make a pot of coffee but when he turned on the water, nothing came out. After checking some things, he realized that the pipes had frozen. He woke everyone up and had the children pack what they needed for school that day. He explained that they could get ready for school at their grandma's house, and that she would drive them to school.

That evening David tried to thaw out the pipes by putting a space heater in front of the kitchen and bathroom sinks. With all his efforts, there was still no water flowing into the sink. After discussing what they should do, David and Sandra decided to pack enough clothes for them to spend that Friday night and possibly all weekend, at his mother's house.

Ethel greeted the twins at the door with arms wide open. "Hello my little princesses. Give your grandma a hug! Derek, my goodness! You are almost as tall as I am," she said, wiping her eyes. "Never mind me you two! These are just tears of joy. I'm so happy to see you all, and for us to be able to spend time together. Just look at you, Ruthann! You are prettier every time I see you," said Ethel. Sandra cleared her throat. "Pretty as, pretty does," she said, with a smile. Sandra said that every time someone told Ruthann that she was pretty. She didn't want her to become conceited, and was teaching the girls that it is more important to be kind and loving on the inside, than to be pretty on the outside.

"I like your pink couch, grandma. You have so many pretty things," said Miranda. "Yeah. I like all the colorful diamonds on your lamp. They match the diamonds in your dangly earrings," said Marjorie. Derek laughed as he put his arms around the twins. "They aren't diamonds! They are fake Jewels. Aren't they grandma?" asked Derek. She winked at Derek, and leaned down so the twins could see up close. "We will pretend that they are diamonds, okay." she said, as she flipped them to make them shimmer. "May we play your organ?" asked Ruthann. "Yes, but tap gently on the keys, and one at a time, please." instructed Ethel, as she pushed the lid open.

Greg stopped by with pizza for everyone, and a bag of candy for the children. They played some games, and laughed at the funny jokes that Greg liked to tell. He stuttered in his speech from shell shock. The ship that he was on during World War II was hit by a bomb, and it scared him so much that he talked with a bad stutter ever since. He was so kind and lovable, that it didn't matter to any of the family. They loved him just the way he was. The evening went by quickly with all the fun they had together. The children took their baths, and then Ethel tucked them in for the night. David went upstairs to take a shower, while Sandra and Ethel had a cup of tea in the kitchen. "Thank you so much for letting us crash in on you like this Ethel. It looks like we are going to have to hire someone to fix the pipes. David tried his best," said Sandra with a sigh. "Think nothing of it, dear. I am so glad that you are all here. Stay as long as you need to. Greg sure does love you all! He asked me to marry him last night, and I accepted," Ethel said, with a glowing smile. "Oh, that's wonderful news! You two look so happy together. I think it's amazing how he wants to wait on you hand and foot. We all love him too! The children will be so excited when they hear the news. Oh, before I forget, we need to get up early tomorrow morning, to go back home and feed the animals. Our puppy, Coco, is in the bathroom. We left her food and water, but we will need to let her out to do her business in the morning. She has been house broke for a few months. My friend down the road is letting her out for us tonight." Ethel put her hand on Sandra's. "You and David work so hard all week. It's too bad that you have to get up so early on a Saturday. Oh well, I'll get up and make pancakes for the children. They will want to watch the Saturday morning cartoons, I'm sure." Just then, the phone rang. "Oh, who could be calling at this hour!" said Ethel, as she walked to the family room to answer the phone. "Hello. Yes. They are. May I ask who's calling? Certainly, but he is in the shower right now. Yes. Sandra is right here." Ethel put her hand over the receiver. "It's your preacher, Ezra, and he says it's urgent." She handed the phone to Sandra. "Hello, Ezra. How are you?" Ezra cleared his throat. "I'm fine Sandra. Are you sitting down?" Because of the seriousness in his voice, Sandra decided to go ahead and sit down. "I have some bad news. I'm sorry to have to tell you this, but your house is burning down." Sandra laughed. She didn't mean to, but it just came out, because she didn't think that it could possibly be true. "You can be so funny sometimes! Stop joking and tell me why you really called. Is there something you need?" she asked. "I'm so sorry Sandra. It's not a joke at all," Ezra said, softly. Sandra sat silently for a moment to let the news sink in. "Okay, thank you for calling, Ezra. I'll go upstairs and tell David that our house is burning down." she said, still with unbelief. Ethel gasped when she heard Sandra say those words. "Yes. We will meet you there as soon as we can. Alright. We appreciate that. Thank you for praying for us." Sandra hung up the phone and ran upstairs. She stood in front of the bathroom door and hesitated before speaking. She didn't know what words to use to tell David the news about their home. "This must be how Ezra felt when he had to call them with the alarming news," she thought, as she knocked on the bathroom door. "Yes, who is it?" he asked. "David it's me," Sandra answered loudly, so he could hear her through the shower. "Hold on to something in there David! Ezra just called with some very bad news. He told me that our house is burning down." There was silence for just a moment, and then there was quite a commotion in the bathroom. David began yelling instructions to her. He told her to get his shoes and keys and to start the car. When Sandra turned around, she bumped into all four children, who were standing right behind her. They heard everything and begged to go along.

At first the Stewart family was silent, as they headed to their burning home, until a blood curdling scream came from the back seat. It scared David so bad, that he suddenly stopped the car on the side of the road.

Miranda, who screamed, was now crying uncontrollably, which caused Marjorie to join in, not even knowing why. Sandra turned around to look at her. "Miranda what on earth-" Miranda interrupted her. "Daddy and mommy! Remember, Coco is in the house!" she cried. David turned around to look at her. "It will be okay. I'm sure the fireman got her out of the house. Look, you all wanted to come along, so even though you are upset, you will have to refrain from screaming. You could have caused me to wreck the car. Now all of you sit back in your seats, please."

There was silence in the car once again. Sandra was thinking about all the things they would have to replace, and how some things could never be replaced. She treasured the antiques and keepsakes that were her mother's and grandmother's. She hoped and prayed that family pictures and her grandmother's ruby ring would be saved from the fire. David was thinking about his guns and hunting gear. Derek was thinking about his bb gun and his Hot Wheel collection. Ruthann wished that she had taken her first, new Bible with her to her Grandma's. She also hated to lose her fringed suede purse. The twins were quietly crying about their baby dolls.

As David turned down the gravel road to their house, they could see the light from the flames. He pulled into the barn lot lane, and they all stared at their house that was totally engulfed in flames. They got out of the station wagon, and David and Sandra held onto the children's hands. As they walked a little closer to the front yard, they were met by Ezra. He put his arm around David's shoulder. "I'm sorry, brother. They weren't able to save much. By the time the firemen got here, the fire had taken over more than half of the house." David wiped his eyes. "Thank you for being here with us . We are very fortunate that we weren't here. We usually go to bed early, so we would have all been asleep when it happened. Thank God we went to my mom's house. We went to stay with her because the pipes were frozen. I'm even thankful for frozen pipes!" Ezra managed to smile. "Unfortunate things that happen can be blessings in disguise," he stated, patting David on the back.

Derek and the twins were staring at the fire in amazement, but Ruthann sat on the ground with her hands over her face and sobbed. Ezra walked over to her, and helped her up off the ground. "Dear Ruthie, everything will be okay. God will take care of your family, and provide in every way." She wiped her eyes and looked at him. "I just got my first Bible for Christmas, and now it's gone," she cried. "I'm sure that we can solve that problem for you, Ruthie. I know that it was special to you but we can be sure, praise God, that His Word never changes." Ezra gave her a hug, and then walked back over to where David and Sandra were talking to a fireman. A fireman pointed to a heap of things that were piled up by the well house, that they were able to save. He also told them that they lost their puppy in the fire, and that they thought the fire may have started in the bathroom where she was. She may have knocked over the space heater, which could have caused the fire.

They all watched helplessly as the firemen put out the last of the flames. The house was a complete loss. Ezra told David that in the morning, he would send some men from their church to help him rake through things, to see what could be salvaged. He prayed with their family, and assured them that the church would do all they could to help them.

CHAPTER *Twenty-Five*

Brotherly Love

avid and Sandra were up early, and headed to the place where their home was now, just a heap of ashes. Ethel kept the children with her. She wanted to take them shopping for some much needed clothes, and then Greg would take them to play at the park. Sandra reminded Ethel that the girls would have to have long dresses and no slacks.

It was shocking for Sandra and David to see their land without a house. There were four other cars there, and men were already raking through the ashes. They looked through the things that the firemen were able to salvage. There were two end tables, a hat rack, and an old dresser, along with some pans and a few dishes. When Sandra saw the old dresser, she ran to it and opened the top drawer. Her heart filled with thankfulness when she saw that the family photo album and other loose pictures were in it, and weren't singed from the fire. David saw Sandra clutching the album to her chest and walked over to her. "The family album! What a blessing to still have that!" Sandra gasped when she saw what David was holding. It was her grandmother's teapot. She put the album down, and took the lid off the teapot . There inside of it, was her grandmother's ruby ring, where she had put it years ago. With tears running down her face, she put the ring on her finger. "You better be careful dear. You don't want to be excommunicated from the church, because you were seen wearing jewelry," David said, with sarcasm and a grin. Together they laughed and cried from being so full of mixed

144

emotions. "God is so good to us David. He saved us from the fire. He knows the desires of our heart, and he even cares about the small things. I dreaded the thought of losing these two things, and here they are, untouched by the fire," she said, as she picked up the album again.

Their family stayed with Ethel for a week, although many other people in the community offered them to stay in their homes. David put a trailer on their land for his family to live in temporarily, until they could build a new house. Adam and Esther told the Amish people in their church about the Stewarts losing their home due to the fire. All of the Amish in the community immediately gathered things to help meet their needs. They received many beautiful handmade quilts. They were given so many of them, that Sandra had to tell Esther that they didn't have room for any more. The Mennonite church brought them boxes of food and clothing. The children's school collected food and clothing for them also. David and Sandra were amazed with the generous giving from their community, and their hearts were full of gratitude. Ezra's wife, Mattie, gave Ruthann a new Bible that was green. She had asked Sandra previously what Ruthann's favorite color was. Derek was given lots of Hot Wheels from his classmates, because his friend Josh told them that he lost his collection in the fire. Esther gave the Amish dolls to Miranda and Marjorie to keep as their own. The gas station attendant in Westfield, Mr. Johnson, gave them two puppies. The twins named them Tacky and Tuffy.

The generous outpouring of kindness and giving went on for months. The Stewart family experienced how God will meet every need. Many times when they needed something, a neighbor, coworker, church member, and sometimes even strangers would bring them just what they needed, without them ever telling anyone their need. God knew!

CHAPTER Twenty - Six

Why?

Sandra decided to stay up late and read a book until David got home from work. She didn't have to work in the morning so she could sleep in. She worried when he wasn't home, when he said he would be. She prayed that he would be okay, and then she fell asleep. When David got home he entered the bedroom, and knocked into something that woke Sandra up. "David, you are so late tonight! It's two thirty in the morning. You got off work at midnight. What were you doing?" Sandra asked, as she sat up in bed. "We're both tired, Sandy. I'll talk to you about it tomorrow," he said, as he gave her a hug. "David! You smell like you've been drinking!" Sandra was shocked because David was never a drinker. He walked into the bathroom without an explanation. She layed back down and tried to figure out what was going on. She feared the worst, but she turned away from those thoughts and prayed for him, and then drifted back to sleep.

Although things were crowded in the trailer, they kept reminding themselves that it was only temporary. In the morning David fixed a big breakfast for his family. He cooked bacon, eggs, fried potatoes, sausage gravy, and biscuits. He enjoyed cooking occasionally and Sandra welcomed it that Saturday morning. She was amazed that he could make such a big breakfast in their tiny kitchen. After they finished eating breakfast, Derek asked if they could ride their bikes to Westfield to buy some candy at the gas station. David told them they could. He wanted some time alone to talk with Sandra. David and Sandra washed the dishes in silence until they were done. "Come, let's sit down at the table," David said, as he led her to a seat. "Are you going to tell me why you were so late last night?" she asked. "Yes, Sandy. I've been wanting to talk to you since Tuesday night. I have something to tell you, and it's killing me inside. I have to tell you because you deserve to know, and I don't ever want to lie to you. It will hurt you, and I could lose you forever. I've been dreading it, so that's why I went out with some guys from work last night, and had a couple beers. I didn't want to come home to face you with what I have to say." Sandra noticed that his hands were shaking, and he had tears in his eyes. She felt sick to her stomach because she knew in her heart what he was going to confess. With a quivering voice he told her that he had been unfaithful to her . "Why David? When did this happen? Who is it?" she cried. "Sandy, I'm so sorry! It was a couple days after the house burned down. I drove to the Graf family's home to pick up some things that they wanted to give us, to help us set up house again. When I got there Emma was the only one there. We talked and- I'm so sorry! It just happened! I don't know what came over us. I didn't mean for it to happen. It means nothing to me. I mean she is- was just a friend. I don't blame you, if you hate me or both of us, for what we did. I'm just begging you to forgive me. I love you with all my heart and-" Sandra interrupted him. "Just stop!" She stood up and walked to the kitchen window. "How could you do such a thing if you love me? Emma was a friend of mine! Do you realize how this will affect our family? I have been a good wife to you. I work hard, and do all I can to please you!" Sandra was crying and yelling with hurt and anger. "We all go to the same church, David! How will I be able to endure it, when I go there and see her? Does she have feelings for you?" David walked over to her to hold her, but she pushed him away. "No Sandra. We aren't in love with each other. You are my wife! We will not be speaking to each other at church or anywhere. I promise! We will avoid any contact for everyone's sake." Sandra ran outside but David didn't go after her. He knew that she needed to be alone for a while. Sandra ran to the barn, and she dropped down on a pile of straw. She sobbed until she thought she'd never have tears to cry again. "God, why?! I've done everything I could to be a good wife and mother. I obey your commandments. I help the poor and reach out to those who are sick. I try so hard to do everything right so- Why?" She cried, with clenched fists.

A while later Sandra could hear David walking near the barn. Part of her wanted him to come to her, and a part of her wanted him to stay away. Without a word, he picked her up and she let him carry her to the house. "My poor, sweet Sandy. What have I done to you? Please, please forgive me," he cried. She kept silent with her face buried in his chest. "When the children return, I will take them to my mother's. We need the rest of the weekend alone. Will you let me come back, and be here with you?" Sandra nodded, "yes." He gently put her down on the bed and kissed her forehead. "I asked God to forgive me, and prayed that you would too. I don't deserve it, and I don't deserve you. I know that if we try, we can get through this. You are the love of my life. I love you Sandy." She rolled over to face away from him. He quietly walked out, closing the door behind him. She wanted to stay in bed forever. She certainly didn't want the children to see her upset and crying.

Sandra didn't know where else to turn, but to the Lord, so she poured out her heart to Him. "Oh God, I am so afraid of the future. Life can be so painful and so challenging! I can't bear this alone! Help me trust you to get me through this. I need your strength and wisdom. I love David, and I don't want to break up our family. Help me forgive him, and forgive Emma. In Jesus name I pray. Amen.

CHAPTER *Twenty-Seven*

Forgiveness

he day passed by so dreadfully slow. Sandra couldn't get herself to leave the bedroom. She knew that eventually she would have to face the reality of what David confessed to her and move on. She had a choice to make. She could forgive him or not. After thinking and praying, she decided that she would forgive him for being unfaithful. She would hold onto God's promise to be her strength and to always be there for her in her time of need. With His help she would be comforted. Sandra believed that with God's love for her, she could go on. She would keep loving David and be the wife that God wanted her to be. She knew that he was sincerely sorry, and that he truly loved her.

Sandra heard David's footsteps in the hall. He knocked on the bedroom door. "Sandy, may I come in?" She reluctantly answered. "Yes, come in." David sat on the edge of the bed and bent over her. She let him wrap his arms around her. "I love the smell of him, even now," she thought. He smoothed her hair with gentle caresses, and then he lifted her hand that was resting on his chest, and gently kissed it. Sandra let him hold her for a long time, without either of them saying a word. It seemed to give some strength back to her. David lifted her chin so that he could see her face. "Sandy, I'll do everything I can to make it up to you. I will prove my love for you. I hate myself for hurting you!" He buried his face on her shoulder and cried. Sandra lifted his head, and wiped his tears. "I believe that you love me, David, and I still love you too. You said earlier, that you knew we could get through this together. I agree that we can too, but not without God's help," said Sandra, as she wiped his tears again. "Do you forgive me then?" David asked. "Yes. I forgive you, David," said Sandra. She stood up to walk to the dresser for a tissue. "David I don't want anyone else to know about this. Will Emma keep it to herself?" David walked over to her, and put his hands on her shoulders. "Yes. She said that she would. She wants your forgiveness also, but she understands that you and her will not be able to interact at church, or be friends anymore. That would be too hard and awkward for any of us," explained David. Sandra blew her nose. "Yes, David, it would be. We must put this behind us, and not speak of it again. I will not use it against you or use it to punish you." David held her close. "I don't deserve you, my love! You are being so good to me. No one has ever loved me, like you do." Sandra grasped his hands tightly with hers. "Look at me David." They gazed intently into each other's eyes for several moments. The two of them were still one. "You are wrong David. God has loved you so much more than I."

A month had passed since the house burned down. They had everything they needed thanks to the generous giving of so many people in the community. David and Sandra spent several evenings looking over the blueprints for the building of a new house on the property. The children were very excited, and had many ideas of what colors they wanted their bedrooms to be. Derek would finally have a room of his very own. The girls would have their own bathroom upstairs which was going to be very convenient. David wanted Sandra to have the large and wonderful kitchen of her dreams. "No more frozen pipes, drafty rooms, or wringer washers for you, sweetheart. I am buying you a brand new washer and dryer!" David said, excitedly. Sandra smiled as she thought about a brand new big kitchen to make her baked goods in. "I remember when you told me a couple times in the old farmhouse, that you wish you had a bay window, so I am making sure that you will have one! I don't want you to have to carry a heavy basket full of dirty clothes to the basement either, so you will also have a laundry chute, my dear," he said, with a smile. "David, can we afford that?" she asked, with surprise. "Yes, Sandy, we can. I want the very best for you!" Sandra's heart was beginning to heal. She actually felt joyful that day, as they talked about the plans for their future home.

The Beachy Amish, Hershberger's Construction Business, was building their new house. They were very thankful for the spring-like weather that they were having in March. They worked diligently to get the house built as quick as possible. Many men from their Church helped David with a lot of the cleanup work, and with putting in a new sidewalk.

On a warm day in the end of April, two men were putting up some decorative stones. They were working on the outside of the house where the front porch was. At noon they took a lunch break and sat on the edge of the porch to eat. When Mr Hershberger took a sip from his soda can, he felt a sting on his lip. A bee was barely inside the can and he didn't see it. He told the other men that he was sure that he was okay. David and Sandra got home from work and walked over to the new house. Every day they checked to see the progress of the builder's work. Sandra gasped when she saw Mr. Hershberger's face. His lip was three times the size it should be, and his face was so swollen that she almost didn't recognize him. "What happened to you Eli?" she asked. "Oh, I got stung by a bee when I drank from my soda can. It was trying to get a drink too," he said, sounding strange, due to his swollen lip. Sandra took a closer look at him. "You should have gone home, and had Jane put some of the Amish drawing salve on it. I know she would have some on hand. It works wonders. You stay right here. I have a jar of it. I'll be right back," Sandra said, as she rushed off. She returned in a few minutes and applied the drawing salve to the side of his lip, where he was stung. She put a bandage on it, and told him to try to keep it there until the morning.

When the carpenters left for the day, David gathered his family together. He wanted them to take a tour together of their almost finished, new house. He prayed over each room, asking God to bless and protect them. He prayed that their home would welcome all who entered. He prayed that their family would love and respect all of those who entered, and that they would be a testimony to any unsaved souls that would visit.

The Riverview Mennonite Church organized a workday to help the Stewart's move their belongings from the trailer to the new house. It was the first of May and the weather was beautiful that day. The Stewart family was very excited because it would be their first night to sleep in their new house. Sandra helped the girls put new sheets on their new beds. She tucked the twins into bed and kissed them goodnight. "I love our new purple bedroom, mom," said Marjorie. "Me too! It's so pretty," added Miranda, as she reached up and hugged her mother. "I'm so glad that you girls like how it turned out. Now, get some sleep because we have a lot to do tomorrow. We have to empty all of these boxes of clothes, and put them in drawers and in your closet. I love you. Good night."

Next Sandra tucked Ruthann into bed. "I really like how your bathroom turned out. The yellow and orange flowers in the wallpaper really brightens the room. You did very well picking it out, Ruthann. It is such a cheery room, and is sure to wake a person up in the morning," said Sandra. They laughed together because they knew how hard it was to get the twins to wake up every morning. She hugged Ruthann and kissed her goodnight. "Oh, I almost forgot. I'd like for you to help me set things up in the kitchen tomorrow. There are several boxes that I need to unpack that are full of kitchen supplies," said Sandra, as she turned off the light. "Sure, Mom. That will be fun, especially when we decorate the walls with things. The ladies from church gave you so many nice towels, utensils, and other things at your house-warming shower," said Ruthann. "Yes, that was so thoughtful of Rachel to plan it for me. Good night, sleep tight, and don't let the bedbugs bite." Ruthann rolled over on her side. "Mom, I'm sure there are no bed bugs in our new house!"

"Son, I am so happy that you have your very own bedroom and it's about time! You are such a selfless young man, and I am so proud of you! You never complained once, about having to sleep on the sofa bed in the living room, in the old house," David said, with pride. Derek beamed from his father's compliment. "Awe shucks, dad. I didn't mind it at all. It was nice actually. I felt as though I was a night Guardsman. If someone broke in the front door, I'd take him down, and protect you all," bragged Derek. David laughed. "You are a very brave young man too. So tell me what way you had in mind to protect us," insisted David, grabbing Derek's toe that was sticking out from the blanket. "Well, a couple of ways. See my slingshot over there. I had my BB gun too. Oh, and here-" Derek reached under the mattress, "here's your brass knuckles. I had them under my pillow every night." David rolled his eyes. "So that's where they went! I wondered what I did with them," said David, holding out his hand. Derek handed them to his father. "Here, I'm sorry that I took them, dad, but I was going to give them back. We shouldn't need them in this house. I think we should be safe here with the new doors that have locks on them," Derek explained. David put the brass knuckles in his pocket. "It's okay Derek. Just don't get into my things, and take anything again. I keep those as a keepsake because they belonged to my grandfather," said David. He prayed with Derek and hugged him goodnight. "You are in need of a haircut, son!" he said, as he tousled Derek's hair.

Sandra and David fell into bed exhausted from the busy day of settling in their new home. "David, God has been so good to us. We thought the old farmhouse was all we ever wanted, and when it burned down we were devastated. We never dreamed how much more wonderful things could be here with a new house on the property. God took away, and God gave back so much more," Sandra said, putting her arm around David. David put his arm around her too. "Yes, and now instead of an old house that constantly needs repairs, we have a new beautiful house. Like Ezra told me the night the house burned down, God can take bad and make it into good. Our God is such a powerful and mighty God, who protects us and provides for our every need." He leaned over to kiss her goodnight, and she was already fast asleep.

Sandra and David were up early the next morning. After breakfast Derek headed outside to put grass seed around the house, and do other yard work. The twins ran upstairs to their bedroom to unpack the boxes of their clothes and things. Ruthann and Sandra worked in the kitchen most of the day putting things in drawers and cabinets. Derek was assigned to carry boxes of canned goods to the basement, and organize them on the shelves. They worked hard all day long and none of them complained.

Sandra and Ruthann were in the kitchen doing the supper dishes. The sun was setting and it was almost dark. "The kitchen looks so pretty, mom. I'm so glad that you have a nice big kitchen with lots of counter space to make your baked goods," said Ruthann, as she dried a dish. Sandra was standing at the sink, in front of the kitchen window, when all of a sudden she screamed and dropped a glass. Up from the bottom of the window, a bald head slowly appeared again. "What mom?" yelled Ruthann. Sandra was speechless, and with her mouth wide open, could only point at the window. Ruthann screamed when she saw the bald head come up again. She realized that it was her brother Derek, with a scary look on his face. "Derek! What happened to him?!" Ruthann cried. They held onto each other as the head disappeared again. A few moments later, Derek ran into the kitchen laughing so hard that he had tears in his eyes. "You guys should have seen your faces! It was priceless!" he said, bent over with laughter. Sandra grabbed his arm and slapped his bottom. That made Derek laugh even more. Sandra crossed her arms and stared at him in anger. "You scared us to death!" yelled Ruthann. "At first I thought you were some window peeper or something, and then I was horrified when I saw it was you with a bald head!" Ruthann said, with tears in her eyes. "Who did that to you?" Sandra demanded. "I did it, mom," he managed to say, through his laughter. Derek sat down at the table. "Dad told me last night that I needed a haircut, so I thought I would do it myself. It just didn't look good no matter what I did, so I got dad's barber kit and shaved it all off. Now I won't need a haircut for a long time!" Ruthann reached over to feel his head. "You look awful with a bald head!" Ruthann said, wrinkling her nose. Sandra softened her look, rubbed his head, and kissed it. "I'm afraid that your father isn't going to be very happy about this. Now, get over here, and help me clean up this broken glass that's all over the floor," Sandra said, lovingly. Derek was holding his sides from laughing so hard. "Okay, but why would he be upset, mom?" he asked.

David stepped into the kitchen and then stopped abruptly when he saw Darek, and stared at him. Ruthann couldn't tell if his silent stare meant that Derek was in big trouble, or if her father was in shock. Suddenly he burst into laughter. "Derek when you get a haircut, you really don't mess around, do you?" David rubbed his son's bald head with both hands, as they both laughed uncontrollably. "You two are something else! Good grief! Let's just hope that your hair grows as fast as your sister Ruthann's does!" said Sandra. David and Derek headed to the basement sitting room, to play checkers. They could be heard laughing, all the way down the stairs. Miranda and Marjorie entered the kitchen to see what all the laughing was about. Sandra told them that it was because of Derek's new haircut. She winked at Ruthann. The twins ran down to the basement so see him. In just a matter of seconds, Ruthann and Sandra heard screams, and then laughter, from the twins.

CHAPTER *Twenty-Eight*

The Birthday Gift

The Stewart's property looked like a whole different place with the new house, the new paved driveway, and a new fence around the barnyard. It was a warm June day, and it was David's birthday. For a couple of months Sandra had been saving money to buy a used Jeep, that David mentioned he'd really like to have. Every day as they drove home from work, he saw it in the used car lot. She called the dealer and asked if he would let her make payments on it. He agreed that she could buy it on a payment plan. She gave the money to her friend, Janet, at work, and then Janet went to the dealership and made the payments. To surprise David on his birthday, she asked his friend, Kenny, to pick it up and drive it to their home on the day of his party. Kenny thought that it would be funny, if he pretended that it was his own jeep. Sandra didn't like the idea at first, but the more she thought about it, she knew that David would get a good laugh out of it.

There was a lot of fun going on at the Stewart's home during David's birthday celebration. Sandra invited his brother's and sister's family, and a few friends from their Church. A group of children were playing croquet in the front yard. Another group, of mostly adults, were playing volleyball. Rachel was helping Sandra take food out to the tables in the backyard. It was a wonderful place to have a shaded picnic, under the old oak tree. Sandra baked two very large sheet cakes for David. She decorated one with a Jeep, just like the one she was going to surprise him with, and the other one had a deer on it.

A few minutes before the planned time for Kenny to drive into the lane with the Jeep, Sandra and Rachel gathered everyone together on the front porch. "I want to thank all of you, for coming here today to celebrate David's birthday with us. After David says grace, we will have a picnic lunch for everyone in the backyard. When lunch is over, we will have David blow out the candles on his cake. That may require another call, for the fire department to come out here again," said Sandra, with a smile. The guests laughed at that, and one of the men joked that certainly David could blow them out, with all the hot air he was full of. Just then, Kenny pulled into the driveway, in the Jeep. Sandra watched David's expression, as he watched Kenny climb out of it. "Oh good, Kenny made it here for your party. Hey look, David! Isn't that the jeep that you were looking at last week? He must have bought it. Wow! I know you want to take a ride in it. Go ahead, and go now, if you want to. It will give the food line some time to go down, and then you and Kenny can come and join us," said Sandra, doing her best to keep a straight face. David was speechless, as he walked toward Kenny. "Hey there, David. Happy birthday! I'm sorry that I'm late, but I had to go pick up my new car. How do you like it?" Still speechless, David climbed into the Jeep, and sat down behind the wheel. He was trying to wrap his mind around how a vehicle that he wanted so badly, ended up being owned by his best friend. "It's so cool, that it makes a person speechless, huh?" Kenny said, as he patted David on the back. David cleared his throat. "It sure is, pretty cool! You never mentioned that you were looking for another vehicle," David managed to say. Kenny rubbed his beard. "You know, that's the funny thing about it. We were just driving by a used car lot and I saw it there, and I just couldn't quit thinking about how cool it was. I just had to have it! It's one of those cars that you just never want to get rid of. You know, I think I'll keep it forever. Maybe even hand it down to my son and keep it in the family. I know we're going to have a lot of fun in it, that's for sure!" Kenny said, with pride. David was speechless again, and just stared at Kenny. "Are you alright, David? You look kind of pale or something." David shook his head. "I'm okay. Hey buddy, I'm really happy for you," David said, managing a smile. "So let's take a spin around the block. I'll let you drive," said Kenny, hopping into the passenger seat. "Uh, not right now,

Kenny. We better go join the rest of them at the picnic, before all the food is gone. We'll take a spin later," said David, as he got out of the Jeep. "Okay, if you say so," said Kenny, grabbing the keys out of the ignition.

Sandra felt really bad when she saw the look on David's face, as he walked to the backyard. He ate very little, and he asked for the twins' help to blow out the birthday candles. She could tell that his heart really wasn't into the birthday celebration any longer. She decided that he had suffered long enough. She asked for everyone's attention, because she had an announcement to make. "I feel that I need to bring something to your attention. As you all know, of course, it is David's birthday. Something else you all know, is that Kenny has a new Jeep. Now the way I see this is, it's really not fair!" There were gasps, and a very uncomfortable silence. David was horrified. He couldn't believe that she would say such a thing in front of everyone. He stood up and started to say something, but Sandra interrupted. "Those of you who think it's unfair, and think that Kenny should give the Jeep to David, please raise your hand," Sandra said, pressing her lips tightly together. There was cheering from some of the people. It was all Kenny could do not to laugh, when he saw David standing there with his mouth wide open, looking like he was in shock. Most of the adults were told ahead of time that they were going to play this prank on David, so they raised their hands. David thought that Sandra had absolutely lost her mind. He walked over to her and took her hand, and whispered something to her. Meanwhile Kenny spoke up. "Well, he is my best friend, so I guess I should give it to him. After all, it is his birthday," Kenny said, as he walked over to David and handed him the keys. Sandra threw her arms around David's neck, and could no longer hold back the laughter. Everyone joined in the laughter, while David stood there for a few moments with a shocked look on his face. He finally figured out what was going on, and that it was a crazy, but wonderful joke on him. He realized that the jeep was his! He cupped Sandra's face in his hands, and gave her a big long kiss. Their display of affection brought on whistles, hoops, and hollers from everyone. "Thank you Sandy! You really are a rascal, and I love you so much!" He kissed her again. "I'll deal with you later!" he said, with laughter and pointing at Kenny. David had a wonderful time the rest of the day. The children had a lot of fun taking turns riding in the new Jeep with the top off.

CHAPTER Twenty-Nine

Lord Have Mercy

When David's birthday party was over, Ruthann and Derek asked if their cousins, Mark and Christy, could spend the night. Sandra said that they could, but that she was very tired, so they had to be quiet after nine and go to bed at ten. They agreed and were very happy that they could spend more time together with their cousins. They kept their word and were in their beds by ten. "Mark, it's eleven thirty. Being as we aren't sleepy, let's get up and have some fun. If we go outside, we won't wake anyone up." coaxed David. Mark jumped out of bed. "Okay, that sounds great." They quietly tiptoed until they were outside. Mark followed Derek to the station wagon and they got in. They talked and laughed for a while, and then Derek came up with an idea. "Hey, Mark, the keys are in the ignition. I know how to drive, so let's take a drive to the Westfield gas station." Mark shook his head. "No way man! You're only twelve! Your dad will kill us if we get caught!" said Mark, reaching for the doorknob to hop out. Derek turned the ignition. "I'm almost thirteen!" Derek yelled. "Stay in here, and I'll make it worth your while," Derek said, with his head barely above the steering wheel, as he drove out of the driveway. "We are going to be in so much trouble," yelled Mark. "Just sit back, and have fun will you!" Derek said, pushing Mark back in his seat. They got down to the stop sign at the t-road, and a car passed in front of them. "That guy saw us! I bet he's going to turn around, and chase us down," said Mark, nervously. "You're being paranoid. He couldn't see that I was a kid, with our headlights shining in his eyes. This is fun!" Derek said, as he made the car swerve one way and then the other. Mark sat farther back in the seat again, and held onto the seatbelt. "Okay, I'll try to have fun too," Mark said, as he swallowed hard.

When they got to the gas station David parked on the side by the alley. Mr. Johnson usually had his truck parked there, but it was Saturday night and he didn't open on Sunday. Derek turned off the headlights. "This is so cool! We got here with no trouble," said Derek, as he opened the cigarette ashtray. "Yeah! You're a great driver, Derek," said Mark, relieved that they were parked. Derek handed Mark the change that he got out of the ashtray. "Go get us each a coke out of the soda machine over there. I'll stay in the car in case someone drives this way, so I can take off and come back for you when they're gone. We can't let anyone see me driving. If someone comes, run to the back." Mark got out of the car to get the cokes. About the time he put the change in the machine for the first soda, Derek saw car headlights heading their way in the distance. He started the station wagon and took off. He decided that he would drive around the block, and then go back to pick up Mark.

Meanwhile, Mark reached for the first soda from the machine. He figured that Derek took off because he got excited, and that he jumped the gun about the headlights in the distance. The car turned off on another road, before it got to the gas station. All of a sudden Mark heard dogs barking, and they were getting closer. He turned around, and saw three of them heading right toward him. He had nowhere to run and hide, so the only thing he could think to do was to climb on top of the soda machine. He managed to get on top of it before the dogs got there by putting his foot on the lever, and pulling himself the rest of the way to the top. The dogs barked at him and started jumping up on the sides of the machine. Mark yelled, making the loudest and scariest noises he could think of, but they didn't go away. Finally Derek pulled into the parking lot right up to the dogs, and honked several times. Two of them ran off. Mark threw a coke at the third one and hit it on the back. It yelped and ran off also. "Hurry up, and get in the car before someone comes!" yelled Derek. Mark climbed down in a jiffy, and jumped into the car. Derek took off, and drove slowly down a gravel road to take the back way home. "Whew, that was close, wasn't it!" Derek said, laughing. Mark had been crying ever since he climbed the soda machine. "Stop crying, Mark. You're okay. I'm sorry for leaving you, but I thought someone was coming, and I didn't want them to see me in the car. Are you mad at me?" he asked, feeling really bad about leaving Mark at the station alone. Mark sniffed and wiped his eyes. "No, but I was pretty sure that I was a goner back there with those dogs!" Derek pulled over to the side of the road. "You sure were smart to think about climbing on top of the soda machine. I'm really proud of you! Do you want to try to drive the rest of the way back? I'll teach you," volunteered Derek. Mark quickly answered. "No! I'll try it some other time." Derek drove back to the house. After getting out of the station wagon, Derek asked Mark what he'd like to do next. "I'd like to go to sleep. I'm tired, Derek. We told your mom that we'd be in bed by ten remember?" said Mark, feeling bad about not obeying his aunt Sandra. Derek grinned. "I sure do, and we were, weren't we? They didn't say that we couldn't get back up," he said, laughing. That made Mark laugh too. "Hey, thanks for going with me buddy. Remember when I told you that I'd make it worth your while? Well, you can have my slingshot for being such a good sport," said David, as he put his arm around his cousin's shoulder. "Swell!" said Mark, smiling ear to ear. They quietly walked to the bedroom and called it a night.

The next morning, Sandra had a hard time waking the boys up to get ready for church. David tried to wake them up a second time. "Get up boys! Come on!" he said, pulling the blanket off of them. "Awe Dad, can't we just stay home this morning?" Derek asked, yawning. "That's out of the question. You shouldn't have stayed up half the night. Now, get up, and if you give me a hard time, you won't be able to have sleepovers on Saturday nights anymore." With that, Derek got up, and pulled Mark out of bed. "Hey take it easy. I'm awake," he said, stretching. Ruthann and Christy were up early. Ruthann was excited about her cousin going to church with her. She was looking forward to introducing her to her friends, Paula, and Carla.

They all climbed into the station wagon. As David was getting into the driver's seat, he had to put the seat back farther into position so he could sit down. "Have you kids been playing in the car again?

How many times do I have to tell you not to do that?" asked David, aggravated. There was silence. "Well, we are almost at the church. Derek and Ruthann, I know that you usually like to sit with the youth, but I'd like for us all to sit together as a family today," said David. "Sure, Dad," said Derek. "That's fine with me Dad," said Ruthann. David thought that they might distract each other during the service, and not properly hear the word of God. He would make sure that there wouldn't be any whispering, writing funny notes, or sleeping going on during the service. He sat between the girls and the boys so that he could easily keep an eye on them all.

When the church service let out, everyone went their own ways. Derek and Mark went behind the church to talk to the other boys, who were throwing a football back and forth. Ruthann and Christy were talking with Paula and Carla in the church basement. The Twins were visiting with the mothers and their babies in the nursery, and Sandra was in the church foyer talking to Rachel about the upcoming bake sale.

David walked out to the station wagon and got in. No longer did he shut the door, when he heard a knock on the window. It was Emma. David rolled the window down. I have to talk to you David. David looked carefully in the rearview mirror to see if anyone was watching. "What is it Emma? We agreed not to speak to one another." She nervously wrung her hands. "I know, David. I'm sorry, but I have to tell you something. It is a hard thing that I must do. David, I am going to have a child. I have been with no one but you." Emma said, with tears welling up. David couldn't believe that he heard her right. He got out of the car. "You're pregnant? How far along?" he asked. "Yes. I am, and I'm almost five months along. I cannot hide it much longer. Only my mother knows about it. She told me that after today, I should stay home until the child is born. She will tell people that I am ill wIth something, to keep down the gossiping." David put a hand on her shoulder. "I am so sorry that I have caused you pain, and for the shame that is to come. Please, forgive me. Sandy has forgiven us both, and has put it in the past but now- Oh, how will she be able to endure the shock of this news? I promised to always be honest with her, so I must tell her," said David, as he looked around again. Emma wiped her tears. "I understand. I think my child and I should not involve you in our lives. I will keep living in my parents home, and they will take good care of us. You have your family, and I don't want to cause it to be broken up. I pray that I'll meet someone who will help me raise my child, and be a good father to the child in our home. Oh, David, we will surely pay for our sin!" David put his other hand on her shoulder. "God has forgiven us, Emma. We made things right with Him. He will make good, out of our bad actions, in time. You will give birth to a wonderful child, and a child is always a gift from God. I'm not sure how involved I will be in the child's life, but you must believe that I will love the child. I care about what happens to you, but Sandy is my wife and she comes first. I'll pray for you both!" David couldn't control the tears from flowing. He embraced Emma, and whispered again. "Forgive me. Now go, and God bless."

David gazed up towards heaven. "Lord have mercy on us all," he thought, wiping his eyes. When he turned around to get back in the car, he spotted Sandra at the entrance of the church staring in his direction. He wondered how long she had been watching him. He slowly walked over to her and reached for her hand, but she pulled it away. "Gather up the children," she said, as she walked away.

CHAPTER Thirty

Faith

David welcomed the chatter of the children, as he drove home from church. He dropped Sandra off at the house, and then drove to Kirksville with the six children. He told them that Sandra was going to rest at home, while they went to the park and to get ice cream. After that he would take Mark and Christy home.

Sandra tried to take a nap while everyone was gone, but her mind kept racing. She wondered why David would break his promise and talk to Emma. She couldn't get the picture of them embracing out of her mind. She was so sure that he loved her, and that he would never be unfaithful again. She just couldn't make sense of it all. "What would David's explanation be, about the scene she captured in the church parking lot?" she wondered. One thing she did know, was that she couldn't go through the same thing again. If he was being unfaithful, she would leave him. She cried herself to sleep.

Sandra was awakened, when David lay down beside her. "The children will be at my mother's house for the day. I told her that I would pick them up at six," said David, with a deep sadness in his voice. Sandra sat up. "What have you got to say for yourself this time David?" she asked. "Sandy, I put you through a lot of pain by being unfaithful, but I promise you that ever since my confession to you, I have been faithful and will forever be faithful to you. What I am going to tell you now will be a shock. It was to me, but what has been done, cannot be undone." Sandra didn't want to hear anymore. She just couldn't bear to hear what she thought he was going to say next. David had tears in his eyes as he reached for Sandra's hand. "Emma had to speak to me Sandy! If you saw us embrace, I did it only as a friend, to comfort her. Sandy, she told me that she is pregnant," said David, as gently as he could. Sandra wanted to run, and tried to get up, but David wouldn't release her hand. "Sandy! You have to stay! You must listen to me!" he said, holding onto her hand tightly. Sandra tried harder to release her hand from his. "No! I will not stay here, and listen to you tell me that another woman will have your child!" She hit him on the shoulder. "Let me go!" Sandra yelled, with anger. David held on to her even tighter. "I will not! I love you, and I will never let you go!" Sandra was crying so hard that she couldn't speak a word. She quit hitting him, and sunk her head into his chest. He caressed her hair. "Seeing your broken heart is killing me Sandy! What have I done? Will it cause you pain forever?" he asked, as he rocked her in his arms while she cried. "Sandy, I told Emma that I would love the child, but that I would probably not be involved in their lives. I told her that I love you with all my heart, and that your happiness comes first." Sandra raised her head. "It's not the child's fault, David. How far along is Emma?" she asked, wiping her eyes. "About five months. She will not be going to church, or out into the community, until the child is born," David added. "People will talk, David. Everyone will know eventually. Our poor children! What will this do to them?" asked Sandra. "We shouldn't tell them now. Let's wait awhile. Sandy, remember when we decided that we could make our marriage work with God's help? That doesn't have to change. He will help us through this too. I know that it is difficult for you to think this way right now, but Emma is suffering too," David said, with sympathy for Emma. Sandra was silent for a moment. "You should know me better than that, David. I can easily sympathize with her, but I am not sure that I can share you and your devotion, with another family on the side. Will you require that of me?" she asked. David hesitated and then answered. "No. I will not ask that of you. I've asked enough from you already. My devotion is first to God, and then to you. Emma preferred that it be that way also. She lives with her parents, and she said that they will want for nothing. She is in good hands. We need to be aware of any needs that may arise though, and we must also pray for them, Sandy."

Sandra stood and walked to the window. "Maybe someday, just maybe, I will be able to accept the child as part of our family. It's just too much for me to even consider doing right now," she said, turning around to look back at him. "I understand Sandy. Truly I do!" said David, as he walked over to her, and cupped her face in his hands. They gazed into each other's eyes. He saw sorrow and love in hers, and there it was, she saw the love and adoration in his eyes, that told her they still were one.

It was Sunday, and a week had passed since David told Sandra that Emma was pregnant. Sandra's heart really wasn't into going to church that morning, but once she got there, she was glad that she did. Rachel greeted her at the door, and she received hugs and smiles from other friends. They sang one of her favorite hymns, and Ezra's sermon was just what she needed to hear. He preached about the power of God that gives us strength, when we have faith in Him. He used the text in Hebrews chapter eleven. "Without faith, it is impossible to please God." Ezra spoke of Noah's faith when he built the ark, of Abraham when he was asked to sacrifice his son, of Joseph when he was sold into slavery, of Rahab the prostitute, Gideon, Samson, David, Samuel, and other prophets, who through faith, conquered trials and tribulation. She left church that morning knowing that God would turn her weakness into strength if she had faith and let Him. She would hold on tight to that promise! She decided that she would trust God to carry her through, no matter what the future held.